I0609919

WILD ASSES OF THE MOJAVE DESERT

LIS ANNA-LANGSTON

MAPLETON PRESS

Wild Asses of the Mojave Desert
Lis Anna-Langston
www.lisannalangston.com
Copyright ©2023 Lis Anna-Langston – All Rights Reserved
Cover Design & Cover Art Jessica Bell
Mapleton Press
First Edition
South Carolina
ISBN: 978-1-957730-06-6
United States of America
Library of Congress Catalog Number: 2022921271

ALSO BY

For Mark, and that kiss at sunset
&
For Jamie, who loved this book from the beginning

"THE MOST BEAUTIFUL STORIES
ALWAYS START WITH WRECKAGE."

— JACK LONDON

CHAPTER ONE

The summer I left South Carolina, mice took up residence in my car. After three days driving across the country and sleeping at rest stops, paranoid, with all my doors locked, I pulled into another rest stop for the night as a slate gray sky spread before me like a canvas. I propped my feet sideways on the dash and slept through a rainstorm. It was cold and dim, but I was free. I'd been tossing off jackets and shoes and bad timing my entire life but there I was, alone and exhausted, but free.

Six long years had passed since I'd last seen the flat landscape of the desert. Escaping was big stuff, especially since it was from the choices I'd made. Like a monk with an empty rice bowl, I thought I could pay penance to the god of Bad Relationships & Poor Life Choices by denying myself the comfort of a bed. Also, I didn't have any money. Leaving on a whim was a last-minute thing, with barely enough money for gas. My sister was the sensible one, so I landed on her doorstep at four o'clock in the morning. Stella yawned and waved me into her kitchen full of dirty coffee cups. It was a relief to not be in a car, even if my sister was a total slob.

The mice set up house in gifts from my ex that carried the weight of conflict. Things I was too lazy to unpack from my car. Things I was too stubborn to leave behind. From abandoned art, stationery, vintage coats, old mail, Mardi Gras masks, and a prop sword from the movie Alexander, a strange utopia formed in my trunk. Parked in the shade of the desert, mice built a life from junk I was too shell-shocked to leave behind.

Three hundred yards away, inside a cool, air-conditioned room, I set up house in my sister's extra bedroom, certain I had PTSD. I wanted to start over, but false starts followed me from room to room. Like a smooth second hand rolling around the dial, time passed. It didn't heal or fix things. I didn't have a map of my life, just a feeling that connected to a feeling, that connected to a feeling. I'd gone too far out into that wide-open space that turns back on you and howls. I pressed wildflowers into the pages of my favorite Murakami. I was a mess.

I honestly thought I could slip back into town unnoticed and work out a new life plan, but that weekend my sister broke up with her boyfriend and stacked his measly crap on the front lawn. His new girlfriend drove over to pick up his Elvis Costello CD collection. That was an error in judgment, because my sister is a fighter, not a lover. My sister put on her ass-stomping boots, and thus began a new chapter in our lives. The bail bondsman was Dylan Wilde's cousin. After I sprang my sister from jail, everyone knew I was back in the desert. It felt like I was hanging on a cross, except crucifixion heralded the end, and I was certain I'd never even started.

The next day began with a swarm of insects. Beetles. *Because, why not?*

I'd built a deep Jungian nightmare for myself over the last six years. I needed a job. The slow buzz of fluorescent lights above my head pushed me close to insanity. I lie; I was already insane. I just couldn't put my finger on why. Like, how does your life just fall apart? Deep anxiety welled in me every time I thought of letting go. But I had to. That's why I was in the kitchen poring over job sites, listening to the lights buzz, doing career-building exercises when Dylan walked in. Never one for calling ahead, or planning, or even knocking, he just showed up. Dylan was good at showing up.

He'd moved into a trailer out in the desert, eating hash brownies and tracking UFO sightings in a journal he won at a rodeo raffle. It was a small town. Rumors flew constantly. I knew all about that stuff before he showed up in the kitchen. Stella told me.

Back to the beetles, though. The back door that led to the patio and down the narrow strip of gravel to the driveway was crawling with bugs.

I pulled a bag of jellybeans out of my backpack as I stepped aside to let him in the kitchen.

"What's up with the creepy bugs?" He grabbed a handful of jellybeans, immediately tossing the green ones back into the bag.

I shrugged, sneaking a glance at their skinny legs.

"Maybe the heat is bringing them out," Dylan said.

"Do you think we should call my sister?"

"I think if it gets any worse you should call a priest."

He poured himself a cup of coffee and leaned against the counter. "So, are you back for good?"

"No."

"Okay," he said, slowly, raising an eyebrow. "Just passing through?"

"No."

"Skye, what the fuck are you doing here, then?"

I stared at him a minute, wondering where the truth began. "I don't know."

"You don't know?"

"I just—," I didn't know what to say. The mice were living in my car. I'd found them three days before. I couldn't figure out how to tell Stella. Or if it mattered. In the beginning, there was matter and antimatter. It all mattered. Mice and insects seemed like a lot to process, so I left it out. She was gone a lot, and she clearly had her own thing going on. I wasn't even sure if I should tell Dylan.

"Come and hang out at my place. I'll help you gain perspective."

"How?"

"Because I've been seeing some weird things in the sky."

"If you stop eating hash brownies, the UFOs go away," I pointed out.

"Haha, ye of no faith. Seriously, ride out there with me."

It was either stay at my sister's house and obsess over being unemployed or follow my best friend from high school out to a trailer in the desert.

"Okay," I said finally. "Let me get my keys." Because here was the thing: Dylan was weird, but something about the two of us standing in that dirty kitchen made sense, and there was a sharp shortage of sense in my life.

I took the mice with me. Maybe not intentionally, but I knew they were in the car. Also, I was hoping they'd like Dylan's place and climb out. They could catch a ride with me back into the city if the snacks ran out. Dylan loved Cap'n Crunch. He ate huge bowls of sugar-coated puffed peanut butter bliss. It was the only thing he knew how to cook. Pushed hard enough he could be talked into pizza, but only really went for the beer.

Speaking of beer, when he handed me a bottle of brew I asked, "Have you been abducted yet?"

Dylan sighed. "Smartass."

Based on that response, I imagined we'd sit in the desert, drink beer, and stare at the sky until we were too drunk to move.

In my absence, Dylan spent money on decent lawn furniture. With the sun setting over craggy mountains, it was genuinely nice to toss aside the stress of the last six years and enjoy a cold one. Dylan had upgraded his beer taste from domestic to import. With a bag of vinegar and salt potato chips, we sat in the dusty silence of a desert on the verge of night.

"What was that?" I blurted out, watching an object run super-fast out of the corner of my eye.

Dylan snapped his head around. "What? Where?"

I pointed towards a patch of scraggly bushes a few hundred yards away. We both sat perfectly still, holding our breath, watching. Then, again, it ran, darting from one place to the next using the bushes as cover.

I leaned forward, the sound of my chair creaking. "Is that ..." My voice trailed off, waiting for confirmation.

Another dart, but slow enough to make out a form. Beer sloshed in my stomach. Whatever was in the distance stopped long enough for me to get a clear picture. My brow pinched tight. "Is that *Charlie*?"

Dylan launched himself out of his lawn chair, yelling, "Grab that rope."

I pushed the chair back and stood, realizing in one single, sudden motion that I was tipsy, possibly drunk. Dylan ran across hard-packed earth, legs wobbling from alcohol and speed. I looked around quick. A plain piece of rope was on the metal table next to me. I grabbed it and followed, pretty sure all the beer I'd consumed in the last hour was about to be reintroduced to the world.

I did some fast math in my head. "Hey, how old is Charlie?"

Dylan crashed to a stop in a bush and pushed himself upright, blood seeping from scratches on his forearms. "Charlie died three years ago. Of natural causes."

A wave of overwhelming hopelessness seized me. "Then what are you looking for?"

Dylan turned, the last few rays of sunset washing him in an otherworldly glow. He opened his mouth to speak, then stopped. In that silence, I saw what every girl had ever seen in him. The full mouth and magnificent eyes, not dulled by alcohol, but instead dazzling, broad shoulders squared against the moment, perfect hands that held tight to beer bottles but held a future of intimacy, maybe.

He exhaled, arms dropping to his sides. "I keep seeing this animal out here and it looks just like Charlie. Explain that."

"So, you're out here chasing a phantom dog?"

"That's bullshit. It's not a phantom dog. Don't make me out to be a wingnut. You saw it, too. Saw it first, I might add."

A low rumble arrived on the horizon, the ping of rocks hitting the underside of a vehicle.

"How many times has this happened?"

He rolled his eyes and stepped out of the bushes, looking around to make sure the dog was gone. "I don't know. Maybe a dozen. That's why I started keeping the rope on the table."

It was the first time since ninth grade I'd seen Dylan plan for anything. The vehicle was close, and I turned. There, through the dusty windshield, I clearly saw the face of Trevor, squinting over his steering wheel at the two of us standing in the middle of the desert, dirty, a little drunk, with me holding a piece of rope in one hand.

Trevor parked his truck and got out. "Everything okay out here?"

And that was how I reunited with my high school crush.

Dylan rubbed drying blood from his forearms. "Let's keep this between us," he whispered.

The truth was too awkward to convey to outsiders. "Deal," I said.

Trevor watched as we hiked back to the trailer. The sun made its way to the other side of the world. Trevor looked so intense, silhouetted with his mohawk and combat boots. My punk rock cowboy.

"I saw Stella down at the Sav-A-Dollar. She said you moved back."

Trevor caused me to have huge lapses in reason. I'd spent my entire senior year making out with him in the very same truck now parked in Dylan's driveway. Well, there was no driveway. It was a big, empty stretch of dirt, but you get the point. I sat on the tailgate drinking malt liquor instead of making good college choices. The tattoo of a dragon curved up Trevor's neck, and my tongue always went with it. He was one of the last people to still have a lip piercing. A metal hoop I chipped my tooth on. We were like two molecules of dust, full of surface tension. One second in his hands, and I'd change from solid to liquid, evaporating in his palms.

The aluminum door slammed shut behind Dylan, bounced, then hung open.

Trevor glanced at the door. "Is he mad at me?"

The question caught me off-guard. "He lost something," I said, in a stroke of vague brilliance.

Trevor's eyes squinted into the vast expanse of desert. "What could he possibly have lost out here?"

Ready to be done with the conversation and get on to making out in the back of that truck, I said, "His mind."

Trevor laughed so hard he forgot to press for a real answer. Evasion is all about delivery. Dylan came back outside and plopped down in a lawn chair, face glistening, wet hair pushed back off his forehead.

According to the Law of Truly Large Numbers, with a large enough sample, any outrageous thing is likely to happen.

I was thinking about that when Trevor turned around in his chair. "What is that scratching sound?"

Before I even had time to ponder such a question, I knew the answer. The mice. They were in my trunk, performing strange mouse rituals.

Dylan flipped the outside flood lights on and looked around. The rest of the desert was pitch black. I straddled this world of mice and men.

In my attempt to not reveal the mice, I averted my eyes and noticed what appeared to be a wedding ring on Trevor's finger. "You're hitched?"

"Six years."

I choked on my beer. "Who's the lucky girl?"

"Jenny Wormgood."

I wiped beer from my chin. "You married Wormy?"

Dylan walked behind Trevor and frowned. I knew what he was thinking. And trust me, I was trying to find the self-discipline to shut up.

In the distance, I saw headlights. By the sheer speed and wild careening over potholes, it had to be my older sister. Stella skidded to a stop, threw open her door, and stepped out wearing jeans and cowboy boots. I'd never seen her wear anything else. When she was eight years old, Pawpaw took her into a western store to buy a new hat for long days on the tractor. Jeans and boots had been her uniform ever since. No one messed with her in high school, and, by extension, no one messed with me, either. While most girls crossed their legs pretentiously to show off wedges or strappy sandals, skin and pedicures, Stella clomped through life in old cowboy boots.

"Hey," Dylan yelled. "Whatcha doing so far from civilization?"

"I just got outta class, and I need a drink before I melt down."

I turned around to face her completely. "Are you okay?"

"No. I am not okay, baby sister," she said, flopping into a chair.

My heart sped up. "What happened?"

She reached into the beer cooler and sloshed her hand around. "I just got outta class, and I have to write a paper on the Nature of Reality. What the fuck is *THAT* supposed to mean? Seriously, who makes this shit up?"

Dylan glanced at me, suspicious but unsure. Stella was his wild card. Once, in high school, they smoked way too much dope while his dad was at work. They made out on the living room floor to the sounds of the Roadrunner beep-beeping, and Stella still claims the sound of a coyote crashing to the dusty bottom of a ravine is sexually arousing.

Trevor's arms fell open, parallel to the night sky. "That's exactly what we're out here contemplating."

It was funny hearing Trevor use words like contemplating because, even though I was the epitome of a modern girl, I still expected smokin' hot guys to be a little dumb.

Stella glared at him out the corner of her eye and dug her underwear out of her butt, which I knew was a thong, because I lived across the hall and she left her dirty clothes everywhere. "Great. So, what the fuck is the nature of reality, exactly?"

I looked at my sister, ready to save her from herself. "This. These electrically charged particles crackling through the air. The holy grail of neurons firing in our brains. Stars blazing and humming and communicating by pulse and frequency. The circle of us in the desert, at this very moment, with all the conditions lined up perfectly. Things like frequency and distance and speed and light. That's part of the nature of reality. Think of time like a fabric, every moment a thread."

Stella blinked, her beer sweating in her hand. "What the fuck were you doing all those years in South Carolina?"

The truth?

I was working at this quasi-massage parlor out by the airport, while my boyfriend learned to play the guitar. I didn't have to do the old rub-and-tug because I was just a receptionist, but the pay was good, and in the middle of two back-to-back recessions I was kinda grateful to be able to stare at the ceiling and contemplate the nature of reality while men groaned on the other side of thin walls. I also learned to draw my feelings.

Trevor tipped his beer in my direction. "Check out big brain over there."

It sounded like flirting, but I knew I'd be drowning at the bottom of that beer cooler if I made out with another married guy, so I ignored it and went back to the existential crisis of my sister, which was kinda my entire life, since I was unemployed.

That night I dreamed that, two thousand years in the future, scientists carbon dated my memories and determined that my last relationship never existed. It was glorious. A total lie, but glorious.

CHAPTER TWO

I woke up in bed the next morning, the tips of my cowboy boots pointed straight up at the ceiling. I stared at the smooth white paint. I couldn't remember how I got home, only that beer makes me ache, and kinda stupid. I rolled over, wondering how many years had to pass before I was grown up enough to remember not to take more than three bottles from the cooler full of fun.

I kicked off my boots, left my jeans on, and walked down the hall topless. Dylan was sitting on the sofa, pulling a little rake over the pristine sand of a Zen garden. My arms flew to my chest.

"I'll get a shirt," I said, spinning around quickly.

Dylan laughed, "Why bother now?"

"Perv. I thought I was alone."

"We're never alone, Skye."

I snatched up one of Stella's tees laying in the hall and walked back to the living room.

Dylan was in the kitchen by then, opening the freezer. He paused, and even though I couldn't see him, I knew what he was looking at. "Do you know you have a dead squirrel in your freezer? At least, I *hope* it's dead."

"Haha," I said, walking into the kitchen and shutting the freezer door. "It's not a squirrel. It's a chinchilla, and I loved him."

Prying eyes turned on me. "What's going on? Why do you have dead rodents in the freezer?"

"Because I have a hard time saying goodbye. I really cared about him and didn't want to leave him behind. He died on me the night before I left."

"What was really going on in South Carolina?"

I scooped coffee into the filter. "I was dating a drummer from a punk rock band. I also sold acid on the side. I cut the sheets into bookmarks, slipped them into plastic covers and carried them around in library books. No one ever thought to check. No one thought a girl with a passenger seat full of books about French poetry would be a drug dealer. You would have been proud of me. I survived the entire financial meltdown because people were busy avoiding reality."

Dylan exhaled so loud I could hear it over the running water. "I thought you said he was learning to play the guitar?"

"He was. He was in this whole transition phase, writing a bunch of folk music."

Dylan blinked without moving, like one of those strange insects on the nature channel.

I flipped the switch to make the magic beans brew.

"So, you were off with some confused douchebag trying to find himself, while Trevor was back home fucking up his life by marrying some girl he doesn't love?"

"Did he tell you that?"

"She's having sex with some guy at the assisted living facility."

"A patient?"

"Gross. No. Some guy."

This was a TMCBC moment: too much conversation before coffee.

"Do you have any more acid?"

"No. I sold it all in a desperate attempt to get out of there."

"Huh," he said, jamming his hands into his pockets.

"Why are you even here?"

He shrugged. "I drove your car back here last night because I was trying to get Stella to have sex with me."

"Did it work?"

"No." He reached for a coffee cup, then said, "Listen. I want to show you something."

We'd been on a dirt road for a while when the charred remains of a car came into view. Instinctively, I looked out the back window to make sure we weren't followed.

The car was burnt to a total crisp, like it had burned for days. Dylan pulled to a stop a few yards away. The whole scene felt cinematic as I stepped out. The creaking, the charred skeleton of a car, the thump of boots on dry ground. A dusty cooler lay open, a few feet away.

"There's a cooler over here." I tipped it with the toe of my boot. "And it's empty."

"Yeah," Dylan said, walking to the burnt car. "It had tubes of bull semen in it."

Two car doors laid haphazardly in the brush, blown off when the gas tank exploded.

"Bull semen?"

"Yeah, it's quite a commodity, and will allow me to live without bill collectors for a while."

I stared at him under the blazing light. Rugged. Manly. *Crazy.*

"You're serious?"

"Quite."

"Did you know the person in this car?"

"No," he shook his head. "I just found it."

Turning in a circle to illustrate the complete isolation, I asked, "Really? You just happened to find this burnt-out car in the middle of nowhere, with a cooler full of bull semen?"

"It wasn't really a cooler full of bull semen. It's kept in canisters inside the cooler, inside these things called 'straws'. But, yes. You make it sound a little more exciting than it was."

"Okay—," My question was cut off by my inability to actually want to hear the truth. "Dylan, how did you find this place?"

He looked at the car for a minute, his eyes falling to the charred hood, warped and twisted. "Charlie led me out here."

The wind changed course. The burnt smell of plastic assaulted my nose. "Your phantom dog led you to a burnt-out car in the middle of the desert?"

"It was still on fire when I got here, but yes. Something like that."

"Why did you bring me out here?"

He pointed to the other side of the car and said, "Follow me."

I followed Dylan about two hundred yards away and stopped. There, in a small charred hole in the earth, a pink-gold stone glowed.

"Whoa," I backed up. "Is that thing radioactive?"

"I don't think so. If it is, I'm screwed. I've been up close and touched it."

"You touched it?"

"Well, yeah. Anyway, I don't have signs of radiation poisoning."

"*Yet.*"

He actually took the time to make eye contact with me before rolling his eyes.

"Were there bodies?"

"No. Not that I saw."

"Drugs?"

"No."

"Just bull semen?"

He nodded. "Which I'm not saying was legal."

"There's a black market for bull semen?"

"There's a black market for everything."

"Okay," I said, confused. "Where do you think the stone came from?"

Dylan jabbed his finger at the sky in an insistent way, and said, "I think it's a meteorite. And I think it might have hit the roof of this car and ignited it."

"Which explains what?"

Dylan shrugged. "I think this rock is here to help us find meaning in our lives. It landed the night you arrived."

Instead of saying something rational, I blurted out, "Mice are living in my car."

Dylan bent over my trunk, the seams of his jeans straining, and said, "My God, this tunnel system is amazing."

I'd previously noticed the near-perfection of their living arrangements. Which made it even harder to get rid of them.

Dylan poked his finger at a pile of stuffing from a vintage coat. "How long have they been here?"

"I noticed them after I got back, but they could have come from South Carolina. Do you think they'll chew through any wires or hoses?"

Dylan straightened up, backing away from the trunk. "Maybe, but mice are pretty savvy. They've got a good thing going. Mice are opportunists."

"Says the man who has black market bull semen."

He shrugged, dusting his hands off and closing the trunk. "You wouldn't turn your nose up at thirty-eight thousand dollars."

"What?"

"Yep. Listen, there was a sign back there on the highway that said they have beer cheaper than gas. Let's go see if there's truth in advertising."

The inside of the White Tavern was dark and smelled like stale cigarettes and grease. A server came over wearing tight black skinny jeans and an old Van Halen concert tee.

Dylan turned sideways in the booth to stretch his legs out. "Tell me about this beer that's cheaper than gas."

"Dollar eighty-four," the server said, which was, in fact, cheaper than gas.

"Do you have any fries to go with those competitive beer prices?"

It had been a long time since I'd had a burger not made from a Portobello mushroom. Around the corner from my house in South Carolina there was a vegan deli. Jump-starting a new food habit, I ordered a lush, hot, juicy burger. I moaned out loud with the first bite.

Dylan looked up from his double order of fries and raised an eyebrow. "Do you and that burger need to be alone?"

I ignored his comment. "Was there anything else in that car? Anything that might indicate a drug deal gone bad?"

"Nope. Just the cooler and the rock."

"Huh."

Dylan locked eyes with me. "That rock means something, Skye."

The White Tavern was empty except for us, and one other table near the back that looked like kitchen staff. Still, Dylan leaned across the table and whispered urgently, "It's like that scene in Pulp Fiction with the briefcase in the diner."

I furrowed my brow and gagged on a sesame seed. "With Honey Bunny?"

"And Pumpkin."

"What?"

Dylan leaned back and shrugged. "Her boyfriend's name was Pumpkin. Honey Bunny and…"

"I know. I've seen it thirteen times. I'm just wondering why we're out here in the middle of the desert with you drawing comparisons of your life to a film that came out when you were seven years old."

"You—you, you mock me, Skye, but there's a connection."

"Between a film and that glowing rock?"

"Yes." He clasped his hands together firmly and laid them on the table.

"There's no rock in Pulp Fiction."

"It's implied."

"No, it's not."

"Yeah, it is. It's in the briefcase."

"We never see what's in the briefcase."

Dylan squirmed in this exaggerated way and said, "God, use your imagination, Skye. It's a glowing rock."

"Okay. Say it is a glowing rock. What does that have to do with us?"

"It's our time to finally make sense of our lives."

"That's what I've been doing."

"No, you haven't."

I grabbed the ketchup bottle and whacked the bottom. "How do you know that?"

"Because you're here. Right back where you started."

His answer was so simple and earnest, I didn't know whether to kill him or cry. "That's not fair." I looked down at my plate with a strange mixture of surrender and hunger. "What do you think I was doing on the East coast?"

Dylan inhaled and shrugged. "Trying to escape this place and burn Trevor out of your mind with hot yoga and gluten-free buns." He touched my greasy hand and said, "It's not a judgment. Look, I don't know what you were doing out there. You didn't exactly call. But you're here now, and so am I, and I believe this is some kind of strange gift."

"If the rock is so important, why haven't you moved it?"

"Because I think it's perfect where it is."

"Which means you've tried."

"It's really heavy. I'm going to have to dig it out. That's where you come in, old friend."

CHAPTER THREE

S tella drove past Sno Cream Castle on the way to the fortune teller. Cardboard covered the windows and the doors were boarded shut. The sight whizzed by so fast that I turned in my seat. Stella glanced over, and I turned in time to catch a glimpse of her blue, glittered fingernails, chipped in all the right places.

I jerked my thumb. "Is it closed for the season?"

"It's closed for good," Stella said.

"What?" I turned back around. "Go back."

Stella sighed. "We'll stop off after the fortune teller. It's best not to make people wait who know how to cast spells."

My eyes rolled up to the ceiling of Stella's Ford. The upholstery had come unglued and sagged. I touched the soft, gray fabric skimming the top of my head.

Stella pinched up her nose. "I don't want a car payment. Don't make fun of my car while I'm saving up cash for a new one."

"I'm not."

The Sno Cream Castle was a desert tradition, the place to congregate in sweltering heat. In summer, if we played our cards right, we could heckle Daddy into taking us for ice cream at lunch, and orange creamsicles after dinner.

I stared out over the landscape of dusty scrub brush. A lonesome flat went straight to the end of the world. I'd traded flat for flat: the flat isolation of the desert for the flat, low country of South Carolina. I couldn't get my head straight.

Thankfully, Stella had never liked to talk and drive, so we sat quietly until carnival lights on a flashing road sign came into view. In the middle of nowhere, right next to the highway, sat a perfectly square house on a dusty piece of land, with a sign so bright it could be seen from outer space. We passed the mailbox and turned onto a gravel drive.

"How did you find this place?"

"I was lost and stopped to ask directions."

"Have you seen him professionally?"

"Yep. Lots of times. He's been helping me work through some personal shit. He's from New Orleans, and he's gay."

"Does that help him summon spirits?"

"The gay thing or the New Orleans thing?"

"Either."

Stella shrugged, slamming her car door. "Maybe. New Orleans is a weird place. You'll have to ask him."

When you're away from family for six years you forget how obnoxious they can be. Stella walked straight up to the man in the dark purple velvet vest and said, "My sister wants to know if being gay helps you summon spirits."

I actually facepalmed. "God, you have a big mouth."

André was a good sport and obviously secure in his abilities. He extended his hand and said, "Why yes, I do believe spirit summoning is in my blood, and that counts for something. Being gay just makes me more fabulous than other psychics."

I liked him immediately.

A round, well-polished table stood in the middle of the room. One shiny crystal ball sat on top, with a stack of business cards proclaiming him to be André the Great. I *so* wanted that description to be true.

André gestured toward the back room. "If you don't mind," he said, reaching for a small basket under the table, "please take off any jewelry and empty your pockets. I'm really sensitive, especially with rings. I can see their former owners."

I looked down at my hand. "I'd kind of like to know how my grandmother is."

Through a tight smile, he said, "You can set it on the table. I don't think Stella drove you all the way out here for your grandmother."

It was the first time I'd been admonished by a psychic.

André lifted a bundle of sage and set it on fire. "Hold your arms out. I need to purify you with smoke."

And other things you never thought you'd hear a gay psychic say on a Thursday night in the middle of nowhere.

The smoke was acrid and smelled like desert brush. "Did you harvest this yourself?" I coughed.

"Sure did. Under a full moon."

Stella was outside charring her lungs when I stumbled out of my session. A wide expanse of dark rolled away, touched by a night full of stars. I inhaled, pulling the door handle up.

She looked at me, and even though her face was in shadow, I knew the exact look. One formed in childhood. "So, are you going to tell me, or do I have to hassle it out of you?"

"Get in the car," I said, glancing back over my shoulder at the glowing windows. In so much dark, the warm, golden light felt like a strange portal; like I'd been summoned to the edge where two worlds met, to find an answer.

Stella took one last drag on her cigarette, then ground the embers into the dust. "Alright, get in. Time to dish."

Headlights cut a path in front of us as we drove down the highway. I recounted the exact words. "He said I'd get something I lost, and I'd come into some money."

Stella glanced out the corner of her eye as she gulped down a warm soda sitting in the cup holder. "That's odd."

I rolled my window down. "Why?" After years of being suffocated by humidity, dry desert air whipped over my skin.

"Because he didn't tell me I was coming into money."

"He said I'd be married or dead before the end of the year. That I'd have to make a choice."

The car slowed ever so slightly as she let up on the gas. "He said that?"

I nodded. "He said there are two paths, and I will take one."

"Did he indicate which one?"

I shook my head.

Slamming her foot down on the gas pedal, she exhaled, "Fucking André."

Sprigs of weeds with tiny flowers poked up through cracks in the asphalt. Old signs in the windows announced banana splits, and milkshakes with swirls of peanut butter cup pieces. The metal-and-concrete picnic tables were still bolted to the earth, but clearly, something had swooped down and taken the soul of the Sno Cream Castle to heaven.

"I haven't had a decent Cherry Limealicious and order of onion rings since they closed," Stella sighed.

"How does this happen?" I wondered aloud.

Stella shrugged. "You've been gone for a while."

"Not that long." I pinched my nose up, making an ugly face. Honestly, I just wanted to cry. "Well, at least Trevor isn't here making out with someone else."

"You really need to go see him at Golden Years."

I turned in a circle, staring out across the cracked parking lot to the road. "He married Wormy."

Stella dug in her purse, pulling out a fresh pack of smokes. She fired one up, taking a long drag. "You didn't want this life anymore, Skye. I don't know why you're so shocked that it fell apart."

I spun around, pointing a finger. "Don't do that."

She shrugged a shoulder and rolled her eyes. "Do what? *Tell the truth?*"

I was about to blurt out how it wasn't fair, but I'd used that phrase too many times already. "It's not the truth."

"Bullshit," she pointed two fingers with a cigarette nestled in-between. "Don't even try that shit with me. You couldn't wait to ditch Trevor, and you couldn't wait to get out of here."

"It wasn't that—," I stalled for words, or reasoning, or *excuses.*

Stella flicked her ashes.

Eighteen wheelers roared past on the highway, followed by a line of cars. A few minutes later, the rumble faded into the distance, and everything was quiet.

"It wasn't that I wanted out of here. It's that I wanted something more."

Stella leaned against the hood of her car and raised an eyebrow. "You're kidding yourself."

Stella's sarcasm was like a noxious gas.

"How do you know?"

"Because you're lost in the details of your life. Look, ever since you were a little kid you've been terrified of letting go. Remember summers in Wisconsin, when you'd hold onto the rope until it stopped swinging, instead of letting go and plunging into the water."

That was the funny thing about Stella: between the boozing and swearing lived a girl with keen observational skills. Still, "The water was freezing," I said.

She bit at chipped fingernail polish on her thumbnail. "You went away, and some things fell apart. Some things changed. You have to face that, or you'll never be able to move on."

"So, I'm just supposed to accept that Dylan is living in the middle of the desert, in a trailer, chasing a phantom dog?"

Rolling her eyes, she turned and walked to the driver's door. "You're a child, Skye. I'm taking you home."

My eyes soaked in the Sno Cream Castle. Stones rose up at the corners where the picnic tables stood empty. I used to swing a leg over and straddle the concrete bench and Trevor at the same time. Every moment dripped with the possibility of his tongue touching mine. That sweet place where cotton candy met salted caramel and I breathed deep, inhaling the scent of skin, sweat, cologne. How I'd climb on top of him and beg in urgent whispers to have sex, and he'd squeeze my ass and drive me home because, while he'd crossed the threshold of adulthood and left his teens behind, I was still underage, and Daddy kept a shotgun leaned against the bar at home.

Stella slapped the dash. "Spells don't cast themselves. You can ask the mental ward if they'll bring you back here on a field trip. Let's get moving."

I turned away from the storefront, burning the details into my mind. I'd see it again. I knew that much. It was off the highway. I'd pass it again. But I would never dip my fingers into a Sugar Cream Shake again, and that made me ache.

CHAPTER FOUR

"Focus." Stella rounded the corner to the next aisle, out of sight. "We're here for candles, Juju Princess."

She had a point. "But look at this bamboo dish rack!"

"Focus." Stella rounded the corner to the next aisle, out of sight. "We're here for candles, Juju Princess."

She had a point. "But look at this bamboo dish rack!"

"You don't even have your own place."

"Someday I will."

"The proverbial *someday*," Stella said, from an aisle even farther away.

I held onto the bamboo dish rack. Deals like that were hard to pass up.

"What's up, buttercup?" a man's voice asked.

I turned. Dylan stood at the end of the aisle with his hand on a display of air fresheners.

"Hey." My body lightened after a long day. "What are you doing here?"

"Buying matches." Dylan sauntered forward and whispered, "You should come with me."

"I can't. I have to light a white candle and recite prayers the psychic gave me."

Dylan blinked, totally unfazed. "Come with me out into the desert."

Stella popped her head around the corner, waving a white candle in a tall glass jar. "Found them." Her lips twisted into a precocious smile. "Oh, hey. Fancy meeting you here."

Dylan wiggled his eyebrows. "Small town."

Stella walked away. "Aisle three."

In an effort to stay on task, I walked around Dylan and followed Stella. At the candle shelf, she gestured to a display that ranged from white tea candles to twelve-inch pillars. All perfectly wrapped in plastic.

Stella looked at Dylan. "I have to get toilet bowl cleaner."

He leaned in, bumping her with his shoulder. "That's hot."

Stella rolled her eyes and walked off.

"Come with me," Dylan whispered.

I let my index finger trail along the plastic wrap. "You're nuts."

Dylan smacked his lips together. "Hey, doll, you just said you can't go UFO watching because a psychic told you to light white candles and recite a prayer."

That annoyed me. Only because it was true.

Under the light of a full moon, the landscape looked like the surface of another planet. A strange plane of existence. Glass candles clanked in the bag on the floorboard. Shapes rose up from the earth. I had this incredible urge to get out of the car and rise with them. Dylan drove like a maniac, curving and jerking around scrub brushes. He drove the way he lived. In this weird, herky-jerky motion that made everyone carsick except him. *The lucky one.*

"Why the sigh?"

"Did you know the Sno Cream Castle closed?"

"Kinda hard not to notice."

"Why didn't you say anything?"

"We were planning on having that concrete picnic table bronzed for you."

"That's not what I'm talking about. I'm talking about the food, the fact that we all used to meet up there. And now it's gone."

"You and Trevor can still screw on the picnic table."

"It's not always about sex, Dylan."

Jerking to a stop, he jammed the gear into park. "Don't kid yourself. We're adults now. It's *always* about sex."

I looked around and saw the faint pink light and the charred car. We'd come full circle.

I pointed. "You have a loveseat in the back of your truck."

"It's fashion-forward," he said, pulling the cooler to the tailgate.

"Aren't you afraid it will fly out?"

"That's what bolts are for."

"It looks dangerous."

Dylan winked in the taillight. "It is. It folds out into a bed." Pulling sandwiches out of the cooler, he asked, "So, what did the psychic say?"

"That it's darkest before the dawn."

"I hope you're joking."

I took a step back and walked over to the small hole with the pink rock. A campsite for kooks.

"So, what compelled you to drive out in the middle of nowhere and see a *bona fide* psychic?"

"It was Stella's idea. She thinks I'm drifting."

"Huh. Your sister is a weird one."

"My whole family is weird, in case you haven't noticed."

"Yeah, but Stella is like weird with superpowers. This last guy changed something in her. It was a bad scene."

"She could kill a bitch with her mind if she tried."

Dylan laughed. Tossing me a sandwich, he said, "Pimiento cheese, pickles and ham."

Just like Trevor's mom used to make.

"Do you have any chips?"

A bag crinkled in the faint glow. "You think I'm some degenerate who forgets the chips?"

I sat on the tailgate and balanced the sandwich on my knees, pulled the top slice of bread off, dropped a handful of chips, replaced the bread, then smashed it down. "So, do we just sit out here and stare at the sky?"

Dylan popped the top on what smelled like an orange soda. "Oh, the sarcasm."

"I'm serious." I sunk my teeth into a yummy bite of teenage years.

"You're full of heartfelt exchanges and unspeakable truths when we're alone."

The desert under a full moon ranks as one of the greatest wonders of the world. All that light spilling across a landscape of darkness awed me every time.

Dylan tinkered with a portable telescope.

"Why aren't the ladies lined up for you?"

Shrugging his shoulders, he laughed. "Just lucky, I guess."

"I'm serious. What have you been doing out here all these years?"

"Trying to figure out how to get all the things I thought I'd get but didn't."

I turned to face him. "What are you talking about?"

"Don't you remember laying out on the hood of this very truck, watching planes take off, and wanting something?"

"Like a tube of all-day-wearable matte lipstick, or winning a million dollars?"

"Either," he huffed. "Both. At some point in your life, didn't you want something, and weren't you pissed when you didn't get it?"

Clouds passed in front of the moon.

"Okay, I'll bite. Oh, great almighty Dylan Wilde, what do you want?"

I could tell he'd been anticipating the question. "I want to make a connection."

"You're out here trying to find God?"

"God is for amateurs. I wanna find something real."

Headlights cut across our small camp, and my whole body tensed. In the middle of nowhere, people peddled in bull semen and black-market organs. Attached to my kidneys, I felt around in my bag for mace.

Dylan stood and waved his arms in the air like he was landing a plane.

"What are you doing?"

"Making sure Trevor doesn't run over us."

"What?" I stood so fast I actually tripped over my own feet.

"I called him before I went to the store." He shrugged. "I didn't know I'd run into you."

Trevor slammed the truck to a stop and got out, totally hot in the moonlight. The action that vehicle had seen was epic. He handed Dylan a super-sized pack of candy.

Dylan laughed, "What's this?"

"You told me to bring a supersized Kit Kat."

Dylan huffed, digging his phone out of his pocket. "Fucking autocorrect. I wanted a six pack of *beer*."

"I thought it was an odd request," Trevor said, before turning his attention to me. "Hey, Skye. Dylan didn't tell me he had company."

At the unemployment office I was asked to create a list of jobs. I jotted down a few things I thought I'd be good at, in no particular order. Mystic revolutionary. Time traveler. Spy. Karmic credit adjuster. Immortal. Televangelist, if I was possessed with the holy spirit, which I wasn't, but if I were. Galactic private investigator. My mind was flooded with ridiculous, off-topic word glop. Yeah, I said it. Word glop. Noun. What your brain churns out when a hot guy approaches you unexpectedly in the desert.

"I looked for you on MySpace for a couple of years." Trevor broke my train of hopeless job prospects.

"I didn't really join the internet community. It doesn't strike me as innovative. It's more like everyone screaming all at once."

"Huh." Trevor popped the cap on a soda. "Fair enough." A circle of moonlight rose over the back of his head. "You could have called. They still have phones out east, right? The funny ones that attach to the wall?"

Dylan slapped his shoulder, "God, you're good with the guilt."

Trevor took a swig, belched and said, "No doubt."

"Yeah, they have phones, Trevor."

"Huh," he said, so jaded and dismissively the guilt actually worked.

"We're all up and running," Dylan said, in that excited way he reserved for things that genuinely thrilled him.

Trevor stood holding his bottle out to the side. He leaned forward, and the silhouetted image of him looking through the telescope was the sexiest thing I'd ever seen.

He exhaled long and smooth, "The moons of Jupiter."

"You can see the moons of Jupiter through that thing?"

Dylan rolled back on his heels, stuffing his hands down into the front pockets of a pair of 501 jeans he was never going to give up. "Yep. Costs a lot of bull semen to be able to see the moons from this planet."

Trevor relaxed his hand, so just a few fingers still held the long neck of his bottle. I wanted to kiss him right there. To climb up his chest and pound my own until the world fell away, strange and scared. The simplest things transform a common act into a holy moment. The sacred, earthy delight of Trevor's hands on me. All over my body. It made me nuts. In more ways than one. I'd left the desert to get away from those hands. To get away from an uncertain future in dark, back rooms full of heavy breathing and the smell of doughnuts. Convinced I'd never have anything or be anything, I'd run east to escape the very thing I wanted more than anything right that moment.

Dylan rapped on the side of his skull with his knuckles. "Where are you?" He asked.

Inhaling sharply, I pulled my sandwich to my mouth. "Just hungry. Spacey."

Dylan raised a silhouetted finger that touched the moon. "Space is why we're here. And validation."

Trevor leaned down, his cologne filling my lungs. I closed my eyes the way I imagined people do after they fall from a height too high to survive. I felt his breath on my ear, and heard him whisper, "Okay. I'll be the first to say it. I missed you, Skye."

I melted, falling into him like a ship swallowed by a storm.

"Oh, my God," Dylan yelled. "Did you see that?"

The only thing I'd seen was a very clear mental image of Trevor peeling off his clothes in front of me. Which, admittedly, would have been weird if it really happened, because Dylan was standing right there.

Jerking my head to the left, I asked, "What?"

But I didn't need to wait for a reply, because as soon as my eyes followed his hand to the sky, I saw it. A light, bobbing, hovering, illuminated by a backdrop of stars.

"There it is," Trevor whispered, in a way that suggested familiarity.

"What is it?" I kept my eyes locked on the strange, glowing object.

Dylan rolled back on his heels. "*Bona fide* unidentified."

I stared up at the light. "Where does it go?" I asked.

"No one knows," Trevor's arm, strong and long, wrapped around my waist. I quivered into his broad, lean flanks, and the smell of his skin was a rush of sugar-coated candy. I wanted to kiss him then and there, to be pulled onto his lap and straddle his long legs and kiss the mouth I swore I'd never kiss again.

How could I want someone so much, someone I'd originally walked away from? It wasn't like I hadn't had his attention. I'd had his complete attention for years. Maybe that scared me. Maybe I started to wonder what it felt like when you were no longer another person's entire world.

I'd gone away to get on with my life, and the only thing I'd done was loop back around to the beginning, empty-handed and alone. There was quite a buzz in the beginning. A bang. The first time we all met. It's not the same backwards as forwards. It's not simply a reversal of events. We were atoms moving through the void. Elementary particles suspended in sunsets and words we didn't dare utter.

Two glowing lights streaked across the sky in front of us. "There's two of them." I whispered.

The lights glowed amber, then a champagne sparkle color. A raw magic seized the moment, and I shivered. We had all arrived here, alone, together, disheveled, a paradox of oneness. The Second Law of Thermodynamics says the total amount of chaos and disorder in the universe always increases. Unstoppable and magnificent, like Old Testament gods. That moment was living proof.

CHAPTER FIVE

I turned toward the sound of Trevor's voice and realized my eyes were fixed on a point of sky. I just stared, like I'd blacked out with my eyes open. I could see everything around me but didn't know what I was looking at. I blinked, and it felt like my eyelids swooped down over my entire body, then popped up like a window blind, leaving me naked and raw and confused.

"Skye?"

"Yes?" I said quizzically.

"We've got to go."

"Okay." I took a step forward, not knowing where I was going.

A loud creak swallowed the silence. The passenger door stood open, waiting for me.

A second later, I felt Trevor's hand on my elbow and followed the sound of his voice as he said, "You can ride with me."

"Where's Dylan?"

"The lights split off. He followed one set. We're following the other."

My eyes swept across the distance until I saw taillights bobbing and weaving.

"We have to go," Trevor urged.

I climbed into the truck, but it felt otherworldly.

I worried about my candles. Judging by the herky-jerky weave of Dylan's taillights, not much was safe in his presence.

The feeling of waking up from a long nap tingled up and down my arms and legs. It was like I'd blacked out. Seeing the lights sent me deep inside myself, deeper than normal. Putting my chest against the dash, I craned my neck to get a better look at the sky. Two glowing lights streaked in front of us.

"There they are," I said, excited by the race of my heartbeat and surprise in my voice.

"Sometimes there's more."

I turned to see the chiseled features of Trevor's face lit up in the dashboard light. "More what?"

Without taking his hands off the steering wheel, he lifted a finger and pointed. "More lights."

My body bumped and jiggled as the truck sailed over the desert terrain. "Is it military?"

"My cousin works at Luke Air Force Base and says about half of what we see is military. The other half is totally unexplained."

"Aaron joined the Air Force?"

Trevor's nods were more pronounced by the bumping. "Five years ago."

"The last time I saw Aaron he was sleeping 'til noon and telling his mom to get out of his room."

Trevor kept his eyes on the lights. The fact that he didn't look over said more than words. "The world went on without you, Skye."

"Thanks. I keep hearing that."

A vicious fact. One I was starting to loathe. Not because I didn't want to see people embracing new opportunities, but because I'd gone away to get on with my life and the only thing I'd done was loop back around. I'd always maintained that if you go far enough, and look hard enough, you'll find happiness. The very thing that eluded me at every turn, every crossroads, every juncture.

Trevor stopped guilt-tripping long enough to turn to me. "Aaron slips us information."

"Isn't it classified?"

Trevor shrugged. "Him and I get together, have a few beers, and he tells me where to look if I want to find something."

The lights glowed amber.

Heaviness weighed my chest down. I could be so weird with Trevor, and I never understood why. The slightest silence turned into an atomic bomb. I was a nuclear meltdown to his single, perfect flower growing from a crack in the scorched earth.

The lights darted to the left and Trevor jerked the wheel to follow along. Truck tires sailed over scrub brush. A metaphor for my life. Here I was, speeding across the rocky terrain of a planet, searching for what might possibly turn out to be advanced alien life, and I couldn't keep my own life in focus.

I glanced up at the sky until three glowing dots filled the dark.

"Oh my God. There's more," I gasped.

The deep growl of Trevor's voice filled the cab. "Sometimes there are dozens. Sometimes just one or two."

"Dozens? How could that be?"

"How could any of this be?" He asked, in that philosophical way that made me think Trevor was way smarter than he let on.

"What do you mean, dozens?"

Gripping the wheel tight, he said, "I mean dozens. Simple math."

Explaining lights in the sky from a few sources was relatively simple. Explaining dozens of lights with no particular source was harder. Instead of arguing my way through the experience, I turned my attention to the lights. The bumps made it hard. I held fast. As we careened across an open stretch, I swore one of the lights slowed and turned to me, watching.

I gulped back a breath that hung in my throat. *It can see me*, I thought to myself. It can see us out here, charging across the surface of a planet, headlights splitting open darkness, dust rising, hearts pounding, hands shaking. Bracing my forearms against the glove compartment, I leaned into the dash. The light hovered.

In a moment of startling surrender, I knew this thing was alive. Light or not, this thing had intelligence and was watching me. I remembered the twins in fourth grade at Elm Elementary who used to hold hands on the playground and sing, "God is watching us from a distance." Stella thought they were batshit crazy, and started carrying bulbs of garlic, and a bottle of holy water she begged Daddy to buy from LaRue's Mystic Gift Store. Say what you want about spells, those twins wouldn't go near Stella, and she liked it that way.

The light jerked to the left. I jerked with it. After a second it fled right, then stopped. The truck engine roared, the shocks groaned. I locked eyes with the light and didn't look away. It hovered, pulsing like a breath, contracting and expanding ever so slightly. It felt like it was inside of me, alive.

An image of my dad popped into my mind. He was standing in the backyard at the grill. He loved that thing. When he wasn't firing it up, he polished the sides. As the scene played in my head, I realized it was Stella's thirteenth birthday party and I sucked in a huge breath, because I knew what was coming. Daddy's sleeve caught a spark and went up in flames. That was the first shock. The second shock came when Mom dropped the bowl of Jell-O fruit salad onto the patio with a deafening crash and ran for Daddy.

By the time she reached his side her top was over her head, in her hands, beating down the flames climbing Daddy's arm. Standing in the backyard with all the neighbor kids watching, my mom saved Daddy in her purple lace bra and a singed top from Dillard's.

I was in awe. Once Daddy peeled his shirt off there was only a tiny burn that Mom treated with her trusty Aloe Vera plant on the kitchen counter.

Later, when I asked how such a thing could have occurred, she tapped my cheek sweetly and said, "Skye, baby, that's how love works."

To this day I had no idea what she was talking about, but knew she was right.

"Skye?"

"Yes?" I turned, expecting to see my mom holding a platter of hot dogs and fish. Instead, Trevor stared back at me, illuminated by the dash light.

My eyes shot to the sky. A pitch-black canvas spread before me with all the usual suspects. Big Dipper. Little Dipper. Sirius. Cassiopeia.

The outline of Trevor's face was sharp and masculine, his blue eyes shining in the dim light. The truck engine was quiet. Jerking my head around, I realized we were sitting out in the middle of the desert with a dark blue dawn rising.

"What happened?" I whispered slowly. "Where are the lights?"

Trevor shrugged, the scent of his cologne rising from his warm skin to fill the cab.

In his best Obi Wan voice, he said, "The light comes, the light goes."

I looked around again, realizing the only sound was our breath. My hands fell to my lap in confusion and exhaustion. "I thought I was somewhere else."

"We all do."

Gripping and releasing my hands to try and wake up, I asked, "Who's we?"

"Me, you, Dylan."

The seat was hard against my fingers. I knew I was awake. I just couldn't believe it.

Trevor leaned back, his legs falling open in that way that drove me crazy in high school. "Me and Dylan call it 'losing time, gaining memory'. So, where did you go?"

"Well, apparently I was here," I said.

"No, I meant, you saw something. What did you see?"

I turned sideways in my seat to face him. "How do you know that I saw something?"

"Because it happened to me and Dylan. So, where did it take you?"

I inhaled, worried I was stepping into a kind of crazy I couldn't get back from. "The time—," I swallowed, stalling. "Stella's birthday party, when Daddy caught his sleeve on fire."

Trevor smiled, big and broad. Even in the dark I could see it. Captivating. Alluring. His smile was like a magnet. "That's a good memory."

"You weren't even there."

"No, I wasn't. But I know about it."

"Everybody knows about it. My mother ran across the backyard, half naked, to save my flaming father."

The latch on Trevor's door clicked. "Come on." He pushed the door open. "Let's get breakfast."

My whole face contorted into a weird shape. "You brought breakfast?"

Glancing back over his shoulder, he laughed, "Well, I didn't make quiche, but I have some food. Come on. We've been in this truck for hours."

I wanted to say, *"We have?"* but knew that made me sound like a lunatic, so I opened my door and stepped out.

The ground was solid under my feet. Nothing had ever felt so grounded and sturdy. I'd spent most of my life in a state of being bounced around, wondering if I'd fly off this huge blue ball barreling through space.

Trevor lowered the tailgate and reached for a beat up cooler.

The sky lit up, a pale fire in the distance. I stood there, shivering. Trevor pulled plastic bags stuffed with sandwiches and chips out of the cooler, then tossed his jacket over my shoulders. I melted a little as he carefully folded back the plastic and handed it over with a regal bow. I couldn't help it. Such a silly thing, but it sent me reeling. Romantic Trevor was all the rage.

The sandwich smelled amazing. Trevor could make a sandwich. Even before I took a bite, I knew exactly what was in-between those two pieces of bread. Turkey, pickles, lettuce, mustard, a thin layer of mayo, and sriracha squeezed in two thin lines across the top.

I sunk my teeth into the sandwich. It tasted like afternoons when Trevor and I successfully skipped school and stayed at his house making out, with Ang Lee movies flickering on the screen in the den. Blinds closed, zippers undone.

My body was tired, but my mind chugged along like a train. I pushed up onto the tailgate. "I think I blacked out."

"For you to do that without Jameson whiskey is pretty impressive."

I bumped my entire shoulder into him, and his deep laugh burst out into the space around us like the sound of a storm, roaring and wild.

"Okay, okay," he said. "That wasn't fair."

I looked at him out of the corner of my eye and smiled. "I'm serious."

He laughed again. "But it was accurate."

I rolled my eyes and bumped my shoulder into him again.

He shifted, standing right in front of me, pushing my legs open. My breath caught in my throat and I coughed. The un-sexy moment. But, God, why on Earth did he have to be so sexy? *Like OMG sexy*. Make me crazy sexy.

Laying a hand on my knee, he said, "Only kidding. That's happened to me and Dylan. It's why we started coming out here together. We'd come to out here in the middle of nowhere and only remember the moments from the past, but not what happened fifteen minutes ago. Frankly, it was kinda scary. Also, for some reason, these experiences drain our phone batteries, or make the phone totally useless. I'm on my third phone. I don't know what's frying them."

I asked in-between chews, "Is that why you have a burner phone?"

He nodded. "Yep."

Trevor was the only guy I'd ever met who said, "Yep." It came from his mom, who was born and raised in Alabama. *Yep. Ain't. Nope.* His mom was one of the smartest people I'd ever met. An Addiction and Substance Abuse Specialist at the treatment center one county over.

"How is your mom?" I asked, thinking I should do something grown up like take her to lunch.

"She's in Evergreen."

I pulled away from him and furrowed my brow. "No."

Nodding slowly, he said, "Yep. She talked me into moving out on my own because she was worried I'd end up being one of those thirty-year-old guys still living with his mom. She worked a lot and wasn't home much. The house was empty. One morning she texted me, said she'd forgotten a bunch of treatment files, and had to go home. She walked in on a burglary. It was three guys. One of them shot her. Three times."

I laid my hands on his hips because I had no idea what to say.

"When she didn't come back to work that afternoon, one of her co-workers called and I drove out there."

Lacking total decency, I asked, "You found her?"

Trevor's chin fell and his mohawk tossed forward, but I could still see his face. A nod was his only answer. I gulped back a passage of time too big to comprehend.

"I didn't know," I said finally.

Raising his eyes to make contact with mine he said, "I know. I told Dylan I wanted to be the one to tell you regardless of how long it took."

I sat on the tailgate with a blazing sun rising to my left, my high school crush wedged in-between my legs, and accepted that I was a total shit. *Like, total shit.* The anxiety I'd felt about leaving settled on my shoulders. A heaviness came over me and I fell forward, letting my head rest in-between Trevor's chest and abs. I felt him wrap his arms around me and put his chin on top of my head. An awkward embrace that felt like forgiveness.

"I'm sorry," I whispered, but it was a hollow sound.

"It is what it is," Trevor said quietly.

"What happened to her house?" My secret Trevor hideaway was gone. Like my entire life with Trevor had been erased. Suddenly, I wanted to lay on the fake zebra rug and let Trevor feed me M&Ms, one by one.

He sighed. "I sold it. Then I married Wormy six months later."

The truth descended on me, overwhelming and complete. I finally understood. He married Wormy because he was reeling, trying to make sense of his life after his mom was murdered. Wormy was his anchor when the world spun out of control. He wasn't in love with Wormy, at least I didn't think so. That changed everything. Or a few things. Or one big thing. At the very least, it got my ego involved, which was probably disastrous.

Trevor inhaled sharply. "Are you tired?"

Feeling the entirety of my second wind, I said, "Not really."

Filling his cheeks with air, Trevor said, "I've got this thing to do and it doesn't require much effort, but it would be kinda cool to not have to do it alone."

We jumped down and climbed into the truck. The fabric of his jeans covered his perfect thighs as he twisted the ignition, turning the engine on. Another metaphor. My engine was totally turned on, too.

CHAPTER SIX

Golden Living was in an out-of-the-way section of town, surrounded by scrubby trees and a few businesses that allowed Trevor to park without drawing too much attention. The truck smelled like fried chicken and hot sauce. Popping the top on my Vanilla Butterscotch Almond Milk Latte, I took a drink of overpriced coffee and asked, "So, why do you have to spy on Golden Living?"

"I'm not," Trevor said, shaking dots of hot sauce all over a fried drumstick, "I'm spying on Wormy."

"Don't you live with her?"

Holding up his left hand, wiggling his ring finger, he whispered, "I'm married to her."

The words slapped me in the face, but the sight of his wedding ring sunk my stomach to the ground. "I know. So, what's up," I said with that weird tone people use to show they don't care when all they do is care.

"I think she's screwing around on me," he said. Juice dripped down his chin. Hot sauce clung to the napkin like blood.

The full weight of his admission rang in my ears. "What do you mean? No, I know what you mean. Why do you think that?"

Trevor chewed and shrugged. "A hunch. I think she's screwing around with this guy we work with. If I'm going to get out of my marriage, then I'd like to do it without losing my ass. Look, I'm an asshole, and I get that part. Her and I were young and stupid and needy, but I've never lied to her or fucked around. Not even a kiss or a hand job. Vows mean something. Her and I can split this thing up and go our separate ways, but she's not playing me. Not like this."

A couple of conflicting emotions gripped me simultaneously. The image of him and Wormy doing it. *Which, gross.* Then, processing the idea that he married someone other than me and had sex. *Because, gross. Also, I am a total child.* Followed by the humbling, electric surge of realization that maybe, just maybe, I'd get to sit on Trevor's lap and kiss him again, someday soon, because he might actually get divorced. That one thought was worth its weight in gold.

"So, while we're waiting, why don't you tell me what brought you back to my doorstep?"

Hardly his doorstep, but I understood. If he was honest enough to let me in on his marriage falling apart, then the least I could do was tell him a story. At 11 AM, in a parking lot, with fried chicken and binoculars, I bared my soul.

"The guy I was living with was married."

Trevor turned in his seat and I felt the sting of judgment. "And you knew?"

Glaring, I argued, "Not at first."

"But at some point, you did know?"

I nodded. "At first, we were just hanging out. Then, one night, he took me to the Noodle House, slipped a quarter into the jukebox to play Journey's "Faithfully," and told me he was married."

"He played Journey for you? What a douche." The pierced ring on Trevor's lip snarled upwards. "And you said?"

I tried to shrug it off with a sigh. "I said I didn't care. And part of me didn't. Then, five years later, I was left wondering why I lived with some guy who was never going to marry me."

Trevor snorted in a weird, dismissive way I'd never heard. "You know, women used to be the honorable ones, the devoted ones. Now, y'all are worse than men."

"Well, look where all that devotion got us." I sunk my teeth into a drumstick to avoid further explanation.

"Yeah, well," Trevor said with a hint of derision, "I learned from the mistakes men before me made."

"Men made mistakes?" I asked, wiping grease from my lips with the back of my hand.

"Your hipster snark does not excuse you."

"All right, Judge Judy, what's with the condescension?"

Trevor sighed and looked away. I was happy to lose the side eye of disapproval.

"A promise is a promise," Trevor said, without looking at me. "Everyone acts like a promise only matters when it's convenient."

"My chinchilla died," I said quickly.

"What does that have to do with what we're talking about?"

"It's part of the whole chain of events that led me back here."

"Well, I'm sorry." He picked up the binoculars and turned toward the Golden Living parking lot.

"About the chinchilla, or me coming back?"

"I don't know, Skye. Some days, I'm sorry about everything."

Imagine this: imagine riding in the back of a limo all the way across town with the hottest guy on Earth. Yeah, that was me. Trevor wore a tux with a pair of black bondage pants and Doc Martens to our prom. Totally swoon-worthy. He kept slipping his index finger down the front of my dress, in-between my boobs, and it drove me nuts.

I slapped his hand away. "Stop. You're going to get me all worked up," I said, doing my best serious face.

"You're already worked up."

"*God, Trevor—*,"

Hannity's drug store stocked chocolate-covered cherries on an end cap by the checkout. For four bucks, you could have twenty-four luscious, sugary-sweet morsels. I loved how they squirted in my mouth, syrup cascading over my tongue. The cherry suspended in the middle. I'm pretty sure Trevor and I were responsible for any profit that company actually made. We built an entire relationship on junk food. Jars of Peter Pan peanut butter with half a bag of M&Ms stirred in, Pop Tarts, Cap'n Crunch, SweeTarts, a rainbow of Skittles stirred into a tub of orange sherbet.

In South Carolina, when I changed my toxic food ways, introducing flax seed and hand-pressed walnut oil into my diet, I found a box of organic pop tarts at the health food store. Instead of sugar, it was sweetened with fruit juice and made with organic wheat. I developed a slow addiction.

It was like putting a piece of Trevor in my mouth. I thought a lot about the body and blood of Christ. How holy people laid a wafer on the tongue. I'd sit alone at my dinette, laying piece after piece of holy, toasted strawberry Trevor on my tongue. A box, sometimes two, sat on a shelf, with a link to my past. I didn't think about it in those terms back then. In those days I convinced myself they were simple food choices. Now, I saw it clearly. A little piece of Trevor in my cabinet. Crumbs I left to find my way home.

We sat in the truck watching the Golden Living facility, and I silently prayed for Wormy to walk out that back door, hand-in-hand with some guy. It was mean, maybe even wrong, but *fuck*, it was real.

Trevor sighed. "Okay. This is obviously a dud. Let me take you back to your car. We'll meet up later."

Translation: We might have a future together.

The fourth time we sat in the parking lot spying on Wormy we had fish tacos, Long Island Iced Tea in a Thermos, and a jar of my favorite pickles Trevor grabbed from the local store.

The designated driver refused alcohol, so I was a little tipsy by the time Trevor, squinting through the binoculars, said, "Buckle up, buttercup. It's on."

Like a dumbass I blurted out, "They're having sex?"

Trevor gave me the side eye. "No. They're in his car. We're going to follow."

Shoving the last of my taco into my mouth to free up my hands, I mumbled, "Okay," and clicked my seat belt.

Trevor had always been a good driver. In between all his reckless danger lived a man of safe extremes. He'd balance on the concrete walls of parking garages and drive a hundred and fifty miles an hour across open stretches of desert, yet never failed to use his turn signal or yield to oncoming traffic. A wild, dangerous bad boy who flossed.

At least he did years ago. I hadn't been blessed with the opportunity to spend enough alone time with Trevor to track his dental hygiene.

Following at a safe distance, Trevor kept his eyes on the road, but laid his hand on my thigh. I wanted him to pull over, put the truck in park, and let me bounce around on his lap naked.

Trevor was my focus obliterator.

To take my mind off sex, I cooked up small talk. "You never told me how all of this started."

"Drunken text messages sent to my phone that weren't meant for me."

Texting while intoxicated. Always a dangerous thing.

"First, she requested to switch shifts, which made me a little suspicious. We'd been working together for years. A seven-to-three slot came open and she took it, explaining it would give her more time in the evenings if she wanted to take a class, but she never enrolled. So, me being the jerk I am, switched shifts, too. That flat out irritated her, and she requested different days off. That made me mad, so I confronted her, and she said she needed a break from working and living with me. That sucked, but I get it. I'm a lot to deal with. Then, about two months ago, she sends me a text late at night that said she couldn't wait to feel my hands all over her body. I was out back with the telescope Dylan let me borrow. I walked inside. She was totally sauced, standing in the kitchen, dropping an empty bottle of wine in the trash can. Quietly, I snuck up behind her, slipped my hands around and under her tee shirt, and when my hands cupped her tits I whispered, 'Neither can I', into her ear. Her entire body went rigid in my hands, and I knew right then that text wasn't meant for me."

Alcohol, fish, and betrayal sloshed around in my stomach.

Trevor could be a *bona fide* asshole, but he didn't deserve that from her or anyone else. And yet I was such a moral-free zone I couldn't even begin to explain where my righteous indignation swelled from. Who was I to judge? Furthermore, who was I kidding? It wasn't judgment. Wormy had her hot little hands on what I wanted.

"So, why doesn't she just leave?"

"Jenny likes a safety net. I think she wants to know this is a sure thing, then she'll jump ship."

"So, you're going to pull the ship out from under her?"

Trevor squeezed my thigh and smiled. "In a manner of speaking, yes."

CHAPTER SEVEN

"Have you even read Jack London?"

"What?" I looked up. Dylan stood in the doorway of the trailer. It was too small to comfortably fit more than one, so I'd resigned myself to sitting outside and working on my tan. "Umm—maybe in school."

"You don't remember?"

"I didn't know there was going to be a test later."

Rolling his eyes, he backed up and walked into the trailer. "Everything is a test."

In the past, I disagreed with Dylan's Zen monk fortune cookie spiritual gangster logic, but now, life did feel like a test. Like I was gonna ace this part, or bomb. Like there was a right and a wrong way to handle this thing with Trevor. A right and a wrong way to watch Wormy throw Trevor to the curb. Like there were winners and losers, and not a single one of us got a participation trophy.

"Come on." Dylan clomped down the cinder block steps, adjusting a ball cap.

Completely mesmerized by the drama in my own head, I must have missed a critical part of the Jack London lecture. "What are we doing?"

Dylan swung an insulated cooler onto the front seat of his truck. "I have one more canister of bull semen to sell."

"I thought you sold it all."

"Nah. You can't unload it all at once. It makes you look desperate."

That simple truth could be applied to anything, semen-related or not.

He pulled a small shaving kit from the open glove box and slammed it shut eight times before the latch finally caught. In his right hand was a thin piece of red ribbon, and what looked like and old dried piece of bark.

"Here," he said, "help me tie this to my arm."

I knew better than to take a dried-up piece of bark without asking, "What is this?"

Dylan fidgeted with the ribbon a second. "The Hessians in Germany believed the heart of a bat attached to your arm with a piece of red string guaranteed success in gambling."

I pulled my hand back. "That's a bat heart?"

"Technically, it's a whole bat."

Which I could see. A flattened, dried bat held in the palm of his hand.

"You killed a bat to guarantee your success?"

Dylan relaxed his jaw and rolled his eyes at the same time, like he always did when he thought I was being dumb. "Don't be daft, Skye. I'm not in the business of killing things. I found it in the desert a long time ago and thought it was cool, so I kept it. Now, it happens to be handy. It obviously died of natural causes. See?" He flipped the dried disc around and I could see that, in fact, it had a peaceful look on its face, even though it had folded its wings up in an awkward position and dried that way.

"Okay, what do you want me to do?"

Pulling his sleeve up, he slapped the top of his bicep, close to his shoulder. A tattoo inked deep into his skin shone in the bright sunlight. A piece of cake inked into his skin with the words, "The cake is a lie."

Turning serious, I looked up, "How long have you had this tattoo?"

"Oh, Skye," he sighed, "just tie the bat to my arm."

Dylan didn't sigh often. Resignation was not a personality trait that dominated his sensibilities. I rode in the cab, separated by a cooler of bull semen, sneaking glances in his direction as we sailed down a smooth, flat highway.

"The guy's name is Billy Ray. He's kind of a good ol' boy, so don't be weird and scare him away. He's probably armed."

I watched a dusty hula dancer with a cowboy hat glued to her head bob and weave on the dash.

"I'm weird and scare people?" I asked flatly.

He looked away from the highway long enough to wink. "You have your charms."

I frowned. "Stop being such a smooth daddy."

Reaching across the cooler he squeezed my knee. "Can't stop smooth, baby."

Ain't that the truth.

Smooth was why I struggled with Trevor. All that hot, deep-voiced, strong-handed, tattooed-torso smoothness.

Before us a highway glimmered in the distance. That was the future. Right there. In seconds, we'd be swallowing up all that distance. Then, that distance became familiar, and was the past. And, in a nanosecond of clarity on the front seat of a truck held together with duct tape, I knew that time branched off from central points. It wasn't flat or linear like the road ahead. You could turn in many directions, paved or not. One thing I knew for certain was that it looped back around. Because all those branches were like a merry-go-round. You could jump off on a certain side, but you'd keep looping back around.

Here I was, back in the truck Dylan bought in high school. A junior at Dawson High when I met him for the first time. Kinda small for his size, but he'd filled out. He'd become a man while I was away. Easy to see now. Still boyish, not exactly mature, but a broad-shouldered man who could lift a bale of hay.

Billy Ray, on the other hand, was a hulk of a man. Barrel-chested in a plaid shirt and dusty jeans, his head was the size of a basketball. He was definitely armed, which made me nervous, because Dylan was so twitchy.

I sat in the truck with the window down. I could hear everything.

"That your girlfriend?" Billy Ray asked.

"Nah, I'm single right now. She's my best friend from high school. Just moved back here." Dylan leaned in and whispered, "Broke up with her boyfriend."

"Ahhh…" Billy Ray said.

I pinched up my nose. I knew he was trying to put Billy Ray at ease, but he didn't have to paint me as a train wreck. The sum total of my existence was more than my dating status.

Or maybe not.

Who knew, exactly? Maybe the fact that I couldn't actually hold a relationship together—with myself or anyone else—was a sign that some of my puzzle pieces were missing. I mean, if completely put together, what did I look like lying flat on a huge dining room table? Was there a castle in the background? A sweeping vista, a ship on the horizon? Was I climbing up the tower to save myself?

I squinted into the sunlight. Once, in an effort to reclaim some ancient part of myself, I'd gone whale watching off the coast of Boston. When the whales rose from the water, a sudden swell pushed up from the boat, and I felt buoyed by the water and the experience, and I burst into tears. I felt close to that moment, but Billy Ray didn't inspire like a whale.

"Well," Dylan said, "it's a bargain."

Billy Ray laid his hand on Dylan's shoulder and said, "Son, I don't believe in bargains. This here is a simple opportunity."

Which brought me around to the politics of cow breeding. Not really something I'd ever put much thought into, to be honest. I could do an internet search later, but it was probably better left to my imagination.

Dylan handed Billy Ray the cooler.

"Okay, thanks," he said. "Call me if you have more purchasing opportunities." Billy Ray opened the door of his truck. A newer model, silver, a lot bigger. I wondered if men's trucks got bigger as they got older.

Dylan hopped in and slammed his door a couple of times to get it to catch. Without hesitation, he pulled out a bank deposit bag Billy Ray must have slipped him while I was whale reminiscing. Inside, stacks of money bound with rubber bands filled it to the brim. They weren't perfect, crisp bills like you see in the movies. These were bills that traveled from pockets and wallets to registers and deposit bags. Those bills had been around the city, state, possibly around the country. The edges were bent, the centers creased. Tens and twenties carefully counted. Still, it was a bag full of cash and, judging by the look on Dylan's face, he didn't care if the edges were bent. Old cash spends the same as new cash, affords the same luxuries, or, in Dylan's case, kept the power on.

"Was that legal?"

Dylan flashed a smile, grinding the gears. "I wouldn't give it a lot of thought, but probably not."

CHAPTER EIGHT

Stella was in the kitchen when we got home. Flipping open the freezer, she pointed at the Don Pablo coffee can and asked, "What is that, baby sister?"

The whole scene stopped me in my tracks. "It's complicated," I offered.

Stella raised her brow the same way evil villains do in comic book movies. "It's not complicated. It's dead."

Okay. So, she had me on that one, but dead and complicated are interchangeable, depending on the circumstances.

Pulling the coffee can out, she popped the plastic lid off. "Why is a dead animal in a coffee can?"

I huffed the way I always did when Stella put the muscle on me. "Because he was in the freezer, but Dylan found him, so I put him in the can."

Dylan nodded smugly.

Stella waggled Don Pablo. "Which explains the can."

I didn't know what to say. Stella lived on take-out. It didn't actually occur to me that she'd dig through the freezer.

"It's just for a little while. Until I figure out what to do with him."

Stella cocked her head. "Daddy knows a taxidermist in town."

Too gruesome to consider, though no less gruesome than burying something in the ground. Death rituals always bothered me. What was the point of life if all we did was end up in the ground? Tethered so tight to a planet we ended up inside it when our spark fizzled. That *really, really* bothered me.

Stella stuffed the can back in the freezer. "Next time, label it."

Point made. Fair enough.

Stepping back, she opened the real bag of coffee and filled the carafe. My family made coffee all day long. Close friends thought coffee made us high-strung. I thought we lived off coffee *because* we were so high-strung.

Flipping the switch to brew, she paused, then asked, "So, have you made out with Trevor yet?"

My entire experience with my sister amounted to me overcoming the feeling of being trapped. A blow to the gut only Stella could deliver.

"He's married," I said flatly.

"So, let me get this straight: you spent six years with a married guy in South Carolina, but are suddenly morally upright when it comes to Trevor's matrimony?"

The hypocrite police was on duty. I didn't know a better way to explain it than by saying, "I like Trevor."

"And you didn't like the other guy?"

"Am I with him?"

Stella shook her head. "Not anymore."

"There's your answer."

Hands on hips, Stella leaned back onto the counter. "Why does everything have to be a courtroom drama with us?"

Good question. The relationship with my older sister and I always felt like a bumpy back road full of potholes. Stella had this unparalleled self-confidence seen only in large land mammals in the wild. She could take on anything. Like, she was the Discovery Channel in action. We all looked upon her with terror and awe, but especially me. She had no fear of anything. Kicking her boyfriend's new piece of ass might have been a challenge for some. Not Stella.

Dylan cleared his throat. It's what best friends are for.

Stella pushed off the counter with an affectionate snort.

Dylan pointed to the carport. I stepped out behind my sister and peered around the corner of aluminum siding. The smooth, oil-stained concrete was crawling with beetles again.

"Holy God," Stella sighed.

"You might want to consult an oracle," he offered.

Stella rolled her eyes. "I don't have time for bug drama. I gotta roll."

"Where are you going," I asked, confused.

"I've got a date with Justice."

"Why didn't you ask me to drive you?"

"I thought you'd be banging Trevor by now."

I appreciated the honesty, but she could have asked. I pointed to her dusty Subaru in the driveway. "Courthouse parking is ten bucks, or you have to run out and feed the meter every two hours."

"It's all good. This is the part where I sweep up my mess. I'll cough up the ten bucks."

Once Stella backed out of the driveway, Dylan turned to me in the front seat of the truck. "So, I was thinking about moving the rock."

I introduced the foreign concept of logic. "What if it emits a poisonous gas?"

Glancing over, he ground the gears into reverse. "That's why I have you."

"Because I am your canary in a coal mine?"

"Because you will keep an eye on me."

"Like babysitting?" I asked, slightly put off.

"No." He slammed his foot on the clutch, shifting into gear. "Don't be daft. You actually get paid for babysitting."

I contemplated the advantages of true friendship from the passenger seat. No real money involved. Just kindness, and good deeds, and the ability to weather anything with another human being. It had its merits, though it didn't pay well. As Dylan drove herky-jerky through traffic, I wondered about the beetles. Their skittering legs. The low ticking sound they made in hordes. I wondered if they had anything to do with the mice. One time in a movie theater bathroom with stars painted on the ceiling, someone had scrawled inside a stall: In the end, everything is okay. If it's not okay, it's not the end.

Easy to commit to with permanent marker. Harder to implement in life.

"There she is," Dylan whispered in a tone I'd never heard before.

Not sure what he was referring to, I glanced over and followed his eyes. In the car in front of us was Wormy and *the guy*. Mr. Cheater Guy. At least I thought it was Mr. Cheater Guy. The sun was so bright the passenger was cast in shadow. One thing was certain: that was not Trevor.

Dylan squeezed the gear shift and gave her the stink eye. "That really burns my ass."

There were two people I knew who said, *that really burns my ass.* My dad, and Dylan. It meant they were really, really pissed.

The last time I'd seen Dylan truly pissed was when some jock in high school dumped a full root beer on his gown after graduation.

Here we were, stuck in traffic, years later, Dylan glaring. If I closed my eyes, I could smell the root beer.

"Maybe they are going to lunch," I offered, trying to smooth his edges. "How can you tell it's him? It's so hard to see through her tinted windows."

His whole body slumped forward as he groaned. "Are you really that dumb?"
"No. I am really that hopeful."

"So, you want her to stay with Trevor?"

"No. I just want her to not be doing something that causes him distress."

"Divorce is the very definition of distress, Skye."

I let my face fall into the palms of my cool hands. "Okay, I get it. I just think there could be less drama."

Dylan dropped back behind a few cars to follow at a distance. "When you marry the wrong girl, you don't get a pass on the bad drama."

True. Still, everyone pointing out that Trevor should have married me made me nervous. I wasn't sure what I wanted or if marriage was in my future. I mean, he could be a booty call, friend with benefits, life partner. I pushed back in my seat knowing I'd taken that one too far. I needed a life before I found a partner, right?

Things no one ever bothered to explain in high school. Or college. Or real life. Where was the manual for being a grown up? Like, who had it, and why was there only *one* copy?

"Oh, gross." Dylan moaned like he was being mauled by a bear.

I looked up and there it was. The proof. The absolute, undeniable proof. Wormy leaned over in the front seat of the car and kissed the guy. On the mouth. With her tongue. *Ugh.*

"Where's your phone?" Dylan yelled, feeling around on the seat.

Pulled into the moment, I looked around and realized that in all the herky-jerky it had fallen to the floorboard.

"Get it," Dylan yelled.

I smacked my forehead on the dashboard. "Ouch." I tried to focus, but my head hurt.

Dylan pushed on my shoulder. "Hurry."

I grabbed the phone and forced myself upright just as Wormy pulled away.

"Dammit." Dylan huffed and groaned. "Argh. Whatever. We saw it. Now we know. Now we know we can get proof."

Up ahead, the car turned right, heading in the direction of downtown. Dylan kept going straight.

"Where are we going?"

"I think I just vomited in my mouth a little. I'm going to need something to rinse out the taste of betrayal before I dig a hole."

I suddenly remembered Jack London saying, "He loved to run in the dim twilight of the summer midnights, listening to the subdued and sleepy murmurs of the forest, reading signs and sounds as a man may read a book, and seeking for the mysterious something that called—called, waking or sleeping, at all times, for him to come."

And in that moment, I remembered the *Call of the Wild* like some strange foreign land, too far away to even be real.

"Don't mention this to Trevor until we have proof." Dylan jerked the wheel and took the next turn. "I wanna fry her lying ass."

CHAPTER NINE

In my absence, the local Co-Op expanded to a larger building. Still small, but without the staggering price tag of Whole Paycheck. I talked Dylan into the deli.

"What's a chia seed?" Dylan asked, staring up at the chalkboard menu on the wall.

"It's sorta like a flax seed."

"Huh," he said, squinting at the board. "What's that?"

"It's like a pork rind."

Fully attentive, he turned to me. "Seriously?"

I actually scowled. "No."

"Huh," he said. "Then it's totally useless."

The deli clerk stared at us. A guy in a cap and green checkered apron, younger than me. My existential crisis made me notice things like that. I wanted to be smug and think I was better than him, because at least I wasn't stuck prepping toppings for a salad bar, but he was probably the owner, blessed with the gift of knowing what he wanted out of life.

How's that for sweeping judgment?

"Do you two need more time?" he asked, not irritated, but genuinely confused as to why it would take anyone that long to order a smoothie.

"Don't we all need more time?" I asked, trying to be clever.

"Whatever floats your boat," he said.

Dylan wandered to the cheese table. The tragically unhip conversation made me want to be done with the process and leave.

"Strawberries. Vanilla yogurt. Pineapple juice and ground flax."

"Two?"

I'd spent so much time alone in South Carolina that I liked the number two. One more than one. "Yes. And make them large."

Behind me, Dylan said, "Do people really pay twelve dollars for cheese?"

Smoothie Man ignored us. Soon, the sound of a blender drowned out Dylan's jabs at pretentiousness. I took him to the cereal aisle with the fortitude of a Christian missionary.

Pointing at a box of whole grain, fruit-juice-sweetened cereal, I offered, "You should try this. It's my favorite."

Dylan curled his lip the way Elvis did before singing songs of heartbreak. "What is that?" Leaning forward, he stared at it like it was an alien covered in ooze. "How do I even let you talk me into these things?"

"It's cereal. Your favorite food."

Grabbing the box, he flipped it around, reading the ingredients. "This is like eating chopped shrubs. Remember those super-thick shrubs at my Nana's house? The ones so dense we could hide? Someone dried them and put them in a box. I bet if we plant this cereal it will grow into shrubs."

"Smartass." I snatched the box out of his hand and dropped it in the basket.

"Why are we even here?"

"Because you said you wanted something to drink, and because we can't keep gorging on burgers and fries."

"Grease. The phantom food group."

The dried bat fell from his arm and smacked the floor.

"See, even your good luck talisman doesn't want anything to do with you when you're mocking my hippie diet."

You'd think something that old would have shattered into a million pieces. Instead, it lay, whole and dead, on the tile. Dylan swooped down and grabbed the bat.

"Two Celestial Bliss smoothies are up," the deli clerk yelled.

"Come on," I said, sure my best friend would come around after a good vegan Rueben.

Sun blazed across the parking lot. Dylan took a huge drink of his smoothie, then pinched up his entire face. "You said this would taste like ice cream."

Before I could even respond, he walked next door to the gas station. By the time I caught up he was inside, pouring sugar packets in his smoothie.

The cashier stared at his phone, oblivious to us.

"What are you doing?" I asked, watching a mound of sugar form on top of the frozen smoothie.

He didn't even glance in my direction. Tearing paper packets open with his teeth he said, "You owe me a six pack, Skye."

"They have a nice microbrew—"

"Miller High Life. Bottles, not cans. And make it two, since you said the word microbrew."

There was that number again.

Two.

Not one.

One plus one.

The first thing Dylan said to Trevor when he saw him in the parking lot was, "She tried to give me a microbrew."

"I'm sorry," Trevor said with every ounce of sincerity you'd imagine from that kind of sarcasm.

"Is this all you do? Drive around and meet each other in parking lots?"

"You got a better idea?"

The truth was, I didn't. I'd just come from a world, false or not, where everyone had big plans. Everyone wanted to be a rock star. Everyone was on the verge of their next huge start-up. Everyone's clothes were perfect. It was exhausting.

Me? I was standing in the parking lot of a discount store in the desert, staring at my ex-boyfriend wearing knee-high socks, cut off shorts, and combat boots.

"What are we doing," I asked, trying to nudge my future forward.

For such a wayward girl, I'd become incredibly interested in my future. If not my actual future, the notion thereof.

Trevor swapped gear from Dylan's truck to his, presumably because his was bigger. "Aaron gives us coordinates of unexplained sightings."

"We should move to Alaska and build a cabin," Dylan said, totally off topic.

"Good long-term goal." Trevor hoisted a cooler into the back of his truck.

"I still don't completely understand what we are doing," I said.

Dylan dropped his sunglasses to the end of his nose and winked. "We're digging up a rock. It's not a metaphor."

"What are we trying to find exactly? Proof of alien life?"

"Forget proof of life," Dylan said loudly. I knew by the tone that he wasn't just well-versed, he was passionate about the subject. "Don't you want proof that there's more to this life than outdoor shopping malls and pretentious landscaping?"

"Isn't landscaping by its very definition pretentious?" I asked.

"Now you're talking."

"So, you want to prove the sole purpose of existence is not to match your furniture?" I ventured.

"I want the sole purpose of my existence to not be purchased with a credit card."

It was pretty obvious Dylan would never sell his soul for Swedish furniture.

I asked the question no one had asked yet. "What if we get out there and find out that everything is real? Faith, death, love, eternal life, magic. Like an explosion of contradictions happening all at once."

"Sign me up," Dylan said.

I'd never been first to take the dare. That was Stella. I did not have the God-given gift to look at something and know it for what it was. That was Stella. I had tenacity. Sheer force to go the distance. Too stupid to give up. That's how I justified leaving Trevor. I wasn't giving up; I was going off to find my fortune. Still, staring at him in his cut-offs and combat boots, sun shining through spiky tips of mohawk, I knew my pot of gold was at his feet. I just couldn't figure out how to make that connection.

"Let's go," Dylan said, slapping the roof of the truck.

Because claustrophobia is very real, I always ride on the outside next to the window.

"Okay," Dylan said, driving Trevor's truck, "this is what we're going to do. I looked up some stuff about summoning higher powers."

"I thought we were UFO hunting?"

"Chill, princess. We're doing both."

I glared at him and he clicked his teeth, shooting at me with his finger gun.

Trevor laughed and I elbowed him in the arm. "Don't side with him."

"He's easy to side with, because later I can say I didn't know what he was talking about."

I think I honestly believed at some point that if I was good, and did everything right, good things would come to me. As it turned out, I was taken advantage of, or taken for granted. Either way, taken. And not the cool, I have a special set of skills, Liam Neeson kind of taken.

My phone rang in my purse. A loud, Usher dance club ringtone. Dylan gave me the side eye. I hated side eye, especially with him.

Not recognizing the number, I turned away from prying eyes to answer. "Hello?"

"Skye?"

I glanced up into the perfect blue dome overhead. This world. Our world.

"Yes?"

"Hey. This is André."

I'd never had a personal call from a psychic before. Intrigued, I asked, "Am I in danger?"

"What? Ha! No." Then his voice deepened, and he said, "At least, I hope not."

That worried me.

"Okay, well, what do you need?"

He sighed impatiently, then sort of launched into mid-thought, "I've had a few visions about you lately."

"Are they good?"

"Good and bad are subjective."

Huh. André made me nervous. "Okay. So, tell me."

"I want you to come in. There won't be any charge. You really are special, Skye."

"Why? Because my confusion makes me more fucked up than most people?"

I expected a long awkward silence, followed by a total lie. Instead, he laughed. "You're in transition, Skye. It's a messy, uncomfortable place to be. I'm just picking up on a lot of stuff I can't place, and I'd like to see you."

I wanted to ask him if it would turn out okay, but that sounded desperate. Also, nosy Trevor and nosy Dylan were eavesdropping.

"Okay. When should I come in?"

"How about tonight?"

"I've got some things going on in the evening, but I can come later."

"Later is good. I get a sort of evening rush when people are out driving. Then I have appointments. I know it's late, but could you come at 2 AM?"

Absurd request, but perfect. "Yes, I can be there at two."

Dylan whistled, loud and clear.

"I have to go, but I'll be there later."

"Good," he said, then hesitated. "Does the number two mean anything to you? I keep seeing it in connection with these visions of you."

There it was again.

Two.

One plus one equals two.

So simple, and yet it was advanced math as far as I was concerned.

CHAPTER TEN

The burned-out car was just as cool the third time. There's something intriguing about the fact that collective hordes turned their backs on a building, or fence, or company, or piece of furniture, or another person. Nobody wanted that thing except you. There was promise in that feeling. Promise in the idea that one thing might be made for you and no one else.

Dylan hunched over the dirt hole, staring at the pink, glowing rock like a third-grader staring at a bug.

In an attempt to make meaningful small talk, I asked, "So, Aaron really spotted unidentified craft right here?"

Dylan looked up at me with that same wild look alley cats have when confronted. "The first half of this mission is about transportation."

I'd become too serious. In my attempt to take ownership of my life, I'd taken on other people's problems in order to avoid my own. It bled the fun out of me in a way I didn't notice until that very second.

Still, resistant to change, I cleared my throat and asked, "Transporting what?"

Dylan pushed upright, squinting under the brim of his ball cap. "The rock. I don't want to leave it out here indefinitely. What if someone takes it? I feel like this rock came to us for a reason."

Cue New Age music with harps and flutes.

"I mean," he said, walking around the edge of the hole, "what if this is our chance at destiny?"

"I'm not following you."

Trevor stepped up behind me, his chest against my back. Every time I felt his body, I melted.

"What if this rock is a sign?" Trevor said.

"A sign from who?"

Dylan stretched his arms out wide and, judging by the confidence displayed, I knew they'd had this conversation before. "The cosmos. Intelligent life. Hell, what if time doesn't really exist, and there are parallel worlds, and alternate versions of ourselves left this rock here as a message?"

"What's the message?"

At the edge of the hole, Dylan stopped, put his hands on his hips, and said, "That's for us to figure out."

Which was exactly the kind of answer that made me run screaming from New Age spirituality. "A message is a message. If you write 'help' in the sand, then help comes, or it doesn't," I said.

"In a black and white world," he shrugged.

"This world *is* black and white."

Shaking his head, Dylan said, "No. This world is a complex infinity of choices."

It was amazing how Dylan could make me feel so dumb and so sensible at the same time. "Where did you even learn to talk like that?"

"I did this month-long fast a few years ago and found a box of Deepak Chopra cassettes at the thrift store for ten bucks. I listened to them all day, every day, with this old Walkman my dad had in the garage."

"There was LSD involved," Trevor added for clarification.

Dylan shrugged. "It got a little trippy. Look, I really admire those Christian monks who wandered around the desert, listening for God."

"So, you're listening for God?"

Rolling his eyes, he pulled a spade out of his back pocket and stepped down into the hole. "You're too literal, Skye. The problem you have in life is that you use literal as a defense so you can defiantly reject what complicates your life."

"You're an asshole."

Trevor slipped his arms around me from behind and squeezed. Being in his arms centered me in a way I didn't want to admit out loud.

"Maybe I am," Dylan said, carefully scraping dirt away from the rock. "But you reject mystery, and truth is inside the mystery. And maybe I'm an asshole, but at least I'm ahead in that game."

"And you know that for certain?"

"Yep."

I wanted to punch him in the dick. "So, let me get this straight: you think I'm dodging my life while you're out here digging up a rock sent to you by God?"

Looking up from the hole, he squinted and smiled at the same time. "Something like that."

"So, what's the message, boy genius?"

Dylan reached down and laid his palm on top of the rock. "All in good time, my pretty."

"Feel anything?" Trevor asked.

"It's warm, but it's out here under the sun." He stepped to the side, pushing loose dirt away with his spade. Pink light glowed up from the ground, faint, but in streams.

"Whoa," Trevor whispered in my ear, giving me chills.

Raising an eyebrow, he looked up at us from the hole. "Hand me that box."

Trevor's body backed away from mine, his boots crunching all the way to the truck.

"What if you get radiation poisoning?"

"Then I'll leave you and Trevor a map to where I buried my money around the trailer."

Financially profiting from Dylan's agonizing death held no appeal. "You buried money?"

Trevor swung his arm around me and handed the box over.

With the patience of a deranged archaeologist, Dylan tried to hoist the rock out. It wouldn't budge.

Trevor and I got on our knees. The light was amazing, intense, like it knew me, like it was in fact trying to tell me something. Give me a long-sought answer. Make sense of my life. If not make sense, then at least point me in the right direction. The tattoos on Trevor's biceps popped up as his arms strained. There I was, out at some crash site, sexually attracted to a man in tube socks and Daisy Dukes, who couldn't get a rock out of a hole.

Trevor looked me in the eye and said, "So since we have time on our hands, why don't you tell us the real reason you left the guy in South Carolina."

Maybe it was the blazing light. Maybe I was exhausted from chasing imaginary things that looked real. Maybe I was just tired of resisting destiny.

Either way, I said, "He had a secret Twitter account."

For a minute or two, no one said anything. Dust swirled in the air.

It took Trevor a few minutes, but finally he said, "You're serious?"

I nodded. "Yep."

"Okay." Trevor angled his entire body so he could see my face. "You broke up with some married dude because he had a Twitter account he didn't tell you about?"

"Well, you make it sound stupid, but yes, that's why."

"The fact that he was married didn't play into your decision?"

"Sure, it did. But I was already invested in the relationship before he admitted he was married."

A large tumbleweed moved lazily across the open space ahead.

"So, the social media account tipped your scale?"

"No," I sighed, feeling judged and pinched and a little stupid, all at the same time. "Look, I knew he was married. That was one obstacle, to be sure. People say all kinds of things when they want to get their way. The Twitter account let me know I'd been tragically naïve and stupid. It was a secret he kept from me because he was broken. He didn't want a whole, honest relationship with someone. He wanted an out. Getting to know people online, and debating back and forth, and being flirty, and deliberately keeping it from me let me know that I was never anything more than a distraction. A girl he liked for five minutes. A girl he would never be one hundred percent honest with, because he equated his one lie with freedom." I stopped, sucked in a breath, and forcibly tried to keep the tears welling in my eyes from spilling out. "It was like a booty call that should have lasted an hour, but instead lasted six long, stupid years."

Trevor never turned away. Instead, he stared at me, presumably trying to figure out how to respond to my insanity.

"A lie is a lie," Dylan said quietly.

If we'd been alone, I would have kissed him. Not in a romantic way, but in an *oh my God there is one person on the planet who understands me* way. It made me cry. There were people who knew me, like, really knew me, and I'd abandoned them at the most promising time in our lives for some married douchebag playing folk songs badly on his expensive guitar, who flirted endlessly in PMs to girls that he explained meant nothing. An endless litany of nothingness.

What are you doing?
Nothing.
What are you doing?
Nothing.
I couldn't wait to never do nothing with him again.

"It's dumb..." I whispered, rolling my eyes, feeling the floodgates open and spill down my cheeks.

Slowly, and with such tenderness, Trevor lifted his thumb and carefully wiped away the tears on one cheek, then the other before saying, "I totally get it, Skye. You're all in, or you're not. People leave doors open because they're going to leave by those same doors. I get it."

Over my shoulder I heard Dylan whisper, "Amen, brother."

In all my life I'd never experienced the absolute peace of someone knowing me. I'd never really surrendered to anything. But there, in the most awkward, weird place I could think of, I closed my eyes, leaned forward, and kissed my high school crush.

"Y'all need to get a room," Dylan yelled from outside the truck, laying a tarp inside a box.

A sweeping sun glowed as I straddled Trevor on the loveseat. Behind him, violet crimson bled down to the earth. Dylan knocked on the truck bed. Trevor waved him away with his hand. It was true. We should get a room, and not make Dylan wait for us, but the sheer bliss of getting my wish after all those years was incredible.

Trevor's lush mouth moved against mine so perfectly. His hands on my ass made me quiver. I wanted to be his and his alone, forever.

Tall order, but I didn't care.

Trevor and Skye.

Do or die.

All or nothing.

Dylan knocked again. "Listen, lovebirds. I need some help. This rock is totally working me over."

I pulled my mouth away from Trevor's, to take in breath and perspective. "Okay," I said.

Trevor squeezed my ass tight. "To be continued?" he whispered.

I nodded, feeling my brain rattle around inside like a cartoon character.

"Definitely," I swung my leg over, stumbling out into the desert to deal with the rock.

"It won't budge," Dylan said.

Wedging one foot in the hole and the other knee on the rim, Trevor reached for the rock and pulled. His biceps strained as he clenched his jaw, still pulling. The thing wouldn't budge.

The burnt-out carcass of car stood guard. An eerie reminder of the past. A reminder that sometimes, things go up in flames.

"Well?" Dylan leaned down.

Trevor dug his fingers under the rock and pulled, giving it one last heave before falling back and settling on the edge of the hole.

"I think it's attached somehow."

"Okay. Listen, I've got a shovel." Dylan backed up, heading for the truck. "Let me try."

Trevor pushed up out of the hole. "I don't know, man. I think it's stuck."

I'd been stuck and moved, so anything was possible. I stared down at the glowing pink rock. It had come from somewhere. More than that, it had come a long way, burned through an atmosphere just to be there, right in front of me. Possibly a piece of a planet. The last remains of hundreds of millions of lives. Not just humans, but ants and baby tree sloths. The last and only piece of a puzzle. A piece of a fallen star.

Possibly, the missing piece to my puzzle. That new thought buzzed in my brain. What if Dylan was right? What if this meant something? What if this piece of rock was a unifying force, a puzzle piece, a weird philosopher's stone for all three of us? What if by touching it I could feel the buzz of a nearby galaxy? What if that rock did, in fact, have meaning? What if all my existential angst was total bullshit?

What if our entire existence ebbed and flowed on a bed of meaning so ethereal and strange, we never really understood it because *we were it*? We were the meaning. The meaning was us. Meanings R Us.

In a desperate attempt to grasp onto something solid, I jumped down into the hole, reached down in-between my feet, grabbed the smooth, quartz-like rock with both hands, and lifted it straight out of the ground.

"Whoa," I heard Dylan say, somewhere behind me.

Like a monk with a bowl of rice, I stood cradling it in my hands, though it was super heavy.

It took a minute, but when I finally raised my eyes, Trevor was staring straight at me, mouth open.

"You did it, Skye," he said, quietly.

Tightening my fingers, I celebrated the moment before nodding. "I did it."

The hole wasn't wide enough for two people, but I could feel Dylan hovering.

"What, exactly, did you do?"

I shrugged. "Just grabbed it with both hands."

"Okay, that's weird," Trevor said.

"You're the daughter of Zeus," Dylan whooped, but then jerked his head back, looking up, checking to make sure I didn't have snakes in my hair.

Trevor reached down to take the rock. Suddenly, above our heads, lights lit up the sky. He didn't have to look up to know what was going on. Light from the sky reflected on the ground.

From behind, I felt Dylan's hands slide into my armpits and lift me up.

"It's happening, Skye!" Trevor yelled.

I could kind of hear him, but then there was this sound, this roar, this weird, loud, bone-shaking sound, like a plane taking off. Dust swirled into the air, into my eyes. I squeezed my eyes shut and turned to shake it off. When I opened my eyes, Dylan and Trevor were yelling at each other, necks straining, but I couldn't hear a single word. I tilted my head and looked into the sky. Lights hovered overhead, blinding and flashing.

I looked down at the rock in my hands and, for a split second, I saw myself in the future, like staring into a big crystal ball. I sucked in a breath, trying to figure out if it was real. Then I saw Trevor running for me, yelling, and a worried look on Dylan's face. I didn't feel myself falling, only my eyes closing.

Twenty-eight minutes later, I woke up on the ground.

Dylan crouched over me like a buzzard, with his cargo shorts hitched up, hairy knees near my chin. As soon as I opened my eyes his whole face lit up, like our childhood dog Millie, who was exceedingly happy to see me every time I opened the door. I appreciated Dylan's enthusiasm, but I wanted Trevor, and I almost slipped into a full-blown panic attack scanning the desert, only to realize I was laying in his lap.

"Skye," Trevor said.

"Yes?"

"Are you okay?"

I remembered fainting, and then the lights. I tried to sit up but was too dizzy. My head fell back into Trevor's lap. I tried so hard to ask what was going on, but the words jumbled in my mind like a vocabulary train wreck.

"*Wha happen?*" I finally managed.

Brow furrowed, Trevor leaned down and whispered, "We're not exactly sure."

Uncertainty was not comforting. Radiation poisoning came to mind.

Dylan looked at me and pointed to the sky. "Do you remember what you saw when the lights were directly above us?"

"Yes," because I was holding— "Wait. Where is the rock?"

"In the back of my truck."

"I want to see it."

Walking over, Dylan pulled the box off the tailgate, lowering it to the ground so I could look inside. It glowed a pale, translucent pink in the box, giving off light. Just seeing it made me feel happy.

Before rock.

After rock.

I made a mental note.

"What did you see?" Dylan asked.

"I saw a question. Like it was written in the sky."

"What was the question?"

"*What do you miss?*" I said.

Dylan dug his heel into the dusty earth. "I miss Stella flashing me her tits during Truth or Dare," he said, wistfully.

I turned to Trevor. "What do you miss?"

Holding my gaze, he whispered, "I miss the thing I never had."

Dylan ran his hands over the top of the rock and said, "Smooth. That was fucking smooth."

CHAPTER ELEVEN

Waiting for my sister in front of the courthouse, I shielded my eyes from the sun and watched a couple approach on the sidewalk. Heat waves rippled over the asphalt.

Squinting, I said, "Daddy?"

The man raised his hand to wave and yelled back, "Skye?"

Dylan and Trevor turned to stare.

Nodding, I yelled, "Mom?"

She flashed a smile so bright it literally sent chills down my spine.

"Hey, Mr. and Mrs. D," Dylan yelled.

"What are my parents doing here?" I whispered urgently, looking around for some place to hide.

"Mr. D is here to make sure I have you back by curfew," Trevor snorted.

"They can't see me like this," I hissed, turning desperately to find an escape.

"Like what?" Dylan whispered.

"I don't know," I squeaked. "Unshowered. Unemployed. Confused."

Like a true friend, Dylan threw his arm over my shoulder. "You say that like this is different than any other time in your life."

"Ha, ha," I said, annoyed. "Don't be an asshole."

It had been years since I'd seen my parents. Three years ago, they diverted their RV from the normal route and parked on the sandy ground of South Carolina to worry about me. Stella said they made the trip in case I needed an escape. I did, but pride won that battle. I was not going back to the desert in my parents' RV. Not then, not ever.

Mom squeezed me so tight I could barely breathe, and Daddy slapped hands with Trevor in some weird gang-initiation way that started back when we were all in high school.

"Daddy, what are you doing here?"

Mom stared at me the way people do when they're trying to decide if they should take the ugly, old dog home from the pound.

Daddy pulled me in for a tight, feet-off-the-ground, spinning bear hug. For seconds, maybe tens of seconds, I was lost in the bliss of that swirl.

"We wanted to surprise you," Daddy said in his deep growl of a voice. "And we wanted to make sure Stella is okay."

I didn't know if Stella told them she'd been arrested. I'd assumed, but never confirmed.

"Your sister is so headstrong," Daddy said, plopping me back on the ground.

"*Difficult* is the word you're looking for."

Dylan slapped Daddy on the shoulder and said, "Good to see you, Mr. D."

We were all hugging and handshaking when Stella exited the building.

"Daddy!" she yelled, running straight for a hug.

"How'd it go?" Dad asked.

Stella shrugged. "Pretty good."

"Who was on the bench?"

"Big Jed."

"He give you any trouble?"

Stella laughed. "Why? Are you going to steal his golf balls?"

"No. I'm going to beat him shamelessly."

"Where'd the ex go?" Mom asked.

"Back to Pasadena," Stella said, scuffing her boots on the concrete like a little kid. "I'm done with dudes for a while."

Dylan frowned. "We're not so bad. Just misunderstood."

If Dylan stared at Stella too long, his whole face glazed over, and he went to his happy place. A place where she'd have sex with him and not roast him over an open fire.

They'd eat cereal and draw naked stick pictures of each other in the wild. I could see he was close.

"Listen," Daddy said, "we'd like to take everyone to dinner."

Trevor loved free food. "Count me in."

"It's good to be home. Let's celebrate." Mom said.

I realized he was right, regardless of how uncomfortable it made me feel. I honestly believed everything happened for a reason. Not in some strange, group therapy way, but in the actual magic of life. Granted, it had been in short supply lately.

Reasons and magic.

I spent years running to new experiences that never materialized. The odd sensation of wanting to reconcile the past with the present came over me. All moments of my life added up to the sum total of now. My parents had come home. After years and years of traveling while I was gone, we'd returned to the same place, at the same time. Part of me felt like an idiotic child who just couldn't get it together. Another part of me felt like a warrior, strapping on armor and sharpening her sword. I suspected the real truth was somewhere in the center, and not as deadly.

"Shall we?" Daddy said, gesturing down the street.

Stella pulled a sour face. "I got a thing, Daddy. I—um, I have something I have to do. I've gotta go meet someone. I'm sorry."

Daddy sighed. "It's the price of surprise, I suppose."

Stella bumped into him with her shoulder. "Rain check?"

The restaurant was a shiny, modern building, with sleek glass tables that made me feel like an imposter. My parents' RV was parked in the adjacent lot. I could see it perfectly through the stylish floor-to-ceiling windows. Two love birds were painted on the side in sweeping, airbrushed strokes.

Suddenly I felt like I was going to cry, like a piece of me cracked under pressure. Instinctively, I reached for Trevor's hand, even though I didn't want comfort. I didn't want forgiveness or peace. I wanted to trust someone with my heart, and that was hard.

Mom and Dad made it look easy. I gawked at my parents, holding hands in front of a perfect sunset. Violet, magenta, apricot melted down onto rooftops. An entire world melting into their gooey love affair. I couldn't explain how Stella and I were even related to our parents.

Time happened quickly for everyone, except my parents. Their faces still glowed with rosy smiles, their bodies still leaned into each other, an uncanny ability to always know what the other wanted. Two people with a perfect love affair had spawned offspring completely incapable of lasting, healthy relationships.

"My little bunny," Mom said, squeezing my hand tight.

Crazy bunny, who couldn't figure out what she wanted to do with her life. I wanted to slip back in time, to when she braided my hair and painted my fingernails. But that wasn't going to happen, because while I couldn't stop waxing nostalgic about the past, I was so eager to step into my future I was about to explode. Ironically, I hung in a desert summer, trapped in limbo.

How do you know when the part of your life you want to begin has actually begun?

Totally legit question, right? Where was the starting line, with a person who pulls the trigger and starts the race? Where were the start and finish lines? The chapter breaks? The last sentence on the last page before the new book that is your life begins? My life had been one long cliffhanger that never made sense. It didn't even hang. Moments just fell over the edge of the cliff and went splat, over and over, in an endless Instagram fail.

Dad looked Trevor up and down, "Jesus, son, I love the way you pull an outfit together."

Trevor nodded, "Thanks, Mr. D."

Daddy was a snappy dresser. Always had been. And he loved Trevor.

Long, shiny pieces of metal and marble wed to create a marriage of innovation and tragically hip design. I felt like an asshole. I was having such a hard time with how much the city had changed while I was gone. This had been a strip of boarded-up buildings. Now, it offered pork tenderloin with figs and goat cheese. It was just the kind of pretentiousness I craved in South Carolina. The newness in my old world made me feel like a spoiled brat. People engaged in conversation around me. I was lost in my own world, unable to let go of the last stupid thought I had.

"I'm going to try the fish with the chili lime sauce," Daddy said.

Dylan smacked his lips. "I wonder if I should order two entrees. This place never puts enough food on the plate."

Mom didn't miss a beat. "Order two. We're paying."

Daddy laughed. "We are?"

Mom gave him the stink eye. "We are."

Leaning back in his chair, Daddy threw an arm around Dylan and Trevor. "I'm just so happy to see all of us together again. It's been a while."

I looked across the table and wanted to cry. Where had all the time gone? And for what? Life lessons? *Because experience is the best teacher?*

Dear Skye's brain,

Shut up and order the fish.

If only I could.

Trevor looked at Daddy. "So, what have you guys been up to?"

"Besides being madly in love?"

Knife to the heart.

My parents.

The honeymooners.

"Well, me and Willa went to Williamsburg and upstate New York, Montana, Wyoming, over into Washington state, down into Kansas and Louisiana, up into south Georgia. It's been so good. We have photos."

"I'm a little jealous," Dylan said.

Dad squeezed his shoulder. "You should come along."

A long, long road trip, where we abandon every single thing we've ever known, like how we wake and sleep and cook and dress. Abandon one fear in every new place. Plant it in the ground or blow it away on the wind. Like a kiss, except you hope the fear doesn't come back to you. At each stop we could let go of one thing that no longer serves us. One thing. How easy was that? It didn't require monumental change all at once. Simple change, one mile at a time. A time to abandon all the absolutely childish things I couldn't stop obsessing over. Like the fact that Trevor married Wormy.

I looked across the table. Dylan sipped water. Trevor and Daddy leaned in and talked to Mom. Then there was me. Me with the runaway preschooler brain. I struggled with trust. I struggled with trusting that this was all going exactly as planned. Because if that was the case, then who planned it? Certainly not me. I would have never planned it this way.

Dear Skye's brain,

Shut up.

My sweet obsession with a mohawk relaxed his mouth, thinking. I wanted to kiss him right then. Launch across the pristine table, with the smudgeless glass and the teal napkins, and kiss him. I wanted to be saved by my own childish inability to trust the universe, which was all fucked up by the fact that my parents had returned. I was the baby, *their baby*, and I wanted to sit on Mom's lap and watch Rugrats while Stella did her Sit-n-Spin a hundred million times.

I needed more sleep and less alcohol.

A meditation group.

Herbal tea.

Organic raw honey facial.

Vegan burrito.

A lobotomy.

Sit-n-Spin.

For adults.

On Trevor's lap.

Our server stepped up to the table in his perfectly pressed black tee and skinny jeans, black apron wrapped around his waist. "So, we have a few specials today."

Specials are good.

Dylan finished ordering his second entrée as Daddy reached for Mom's hand and announced, "We're getting married again."

Trevor actually smiled. A teeny smile, but I saw it.

"Where," I asked. "And why?" I was confused. "Do you mean renewing your vows?" Unbelievable. My parents were getting married again, and I couldn't even find a job.

"No," Mom said. "We thought about that, but it sounds so dumb. We don't want to renew our vows. We want the experience of doing it all over again. When you love someone, you want to marry them all over again."

"Right on," Trevor said. *The only other married person at the table.*

"See," Daddy said, "When me and Willa got married the first time, it was magical. The tiny inn, and the candlelight, and the fireflies. But none of you were there to take part in the ceremony, to be a part of that magic. So, we thought, 'What if we get married again and, this time, all of you are present?'"

Dylan shrugged the way he did when he really liked something. "Makes sense."

"We thought so," Mom said, staring all googly-eyed at Daddy.

Dylan polished off the last bit of baguette with maple butter. "You know, I can perform the ceremony."

Daddy shifted in his seat. "Really?"

"Yep. I am a *bona fide* ordained minister."

"Did you answer one of those weird ads in the back of a magazine?"

"Nope. I was ordained by an actual minister three years ago."

"Why?" I asked.

"Because I was helping out at the Eternal Salvation food pantry, and Preacher Roland thought I might be a good representative of the holy."

"You're nuts," I said.

Dylan shrugged. "I ate a bunch of pot brownies and read the Old Testament."

I sat there, blinking. "You're serious?"

He flashed that dazzling smile. "Totally."

I was about to tell him how dangerous it is to mix drugs and religion when, out of the corner of my eye, I saw Charlie the phantom dog sitting on the sidewalk across the street, staring right at us, wagging her tail.

Before I even had time to think about what I was doing, I pushed my chair back and yelled, "Catch her!"

"Take that alley," Dylan yelled to me and Trevor, before turning and running back down the sidewalk.

Trevor grabbed my hand like one of those guys in the movies when they make a run for it. Running as fast as we could past dumpsters and wooden pallets stacked against the walls, he squeezed my hand tight, and I tried to keep up. At the end of the alley we thundered to a stop as a delivery truck rumbled past. I looked left, then right. The truck turned onto the main street. Then, I saw her. Charlie was at the far end, next to a trash can.

I squeezed and pulled Trevor's hand at the same time.

"What?"

"There," I pointed.

Trevor turned and, for a split second, he and Charlie locked eyes. Her eyes narrowed, then widened. She wasn't just a figment, but she wasn't real, either. I was just about to run toward her when Trevor knelt down.

Holding me tight, he let one knee come to rest on the concrete. "Charlie," he whispered.

Charlie had always been a funny-looking dog. Medium sized, black, with her big eyes and huge ears that stood straight up on her furry head. She'd been with Dylan since before we met, and they went everywhere together.

"She wants to tell us something," Trevor whispered.

Kneeling down, I melted into the side of his body. The warm, sweet smell of Trevor. His hard thighs touching mine. His knuckles pressing against my fingers. Suddenly, I was aware of my own breath. Not winded, but sharp, because I'd run down streets and alleyways, my heart beating fast, the way it did when I expected to get something I really wanted.

Charlie stared at us.

"What is it, girl?" Trevor whispered. "What do you want to tell us?"

You don't take the path of fear. You take the path of power. Old fortune cookie saying, but it was so true in that moment.

I was so afraid she wasn't real, but if she was real, what did that prove?

Real versus not real.

And what exactly was not real?

Or real, for that matter?

And why did it matter?

Why was I so afraid that this guy holding onto my hand, talking to an imaginary dog, was going to hurt me? Because that was what made me pull back and run, every time. This deep fear that Trevor would crack me open, make me fall apart, wind me up, turn me lose, dangle me over a fiery pit, and then drop me.

Like I dropped him.

Charlie walked towards us, and every fiber of my being froze. With my eyes glued to her, I watched each paw lift and touch down on the concrete.

At the end of the alley Mom ran by and stopped, backing up.

Charlie glanced over her shoulder.

"You're real," I whispered, so low I could barely hear the words.

Then, just like fog lifting, she disappeared.

CHAPTER TWELVE

A pink glow emanated from the truck bed as Dylan sailed down the smooth stretch of highway. Trevor laid his hand on my thigh. So many things flew through my mind at breakneck speed.

My parents were home.
I'd pulled a rock from a hole.
I'd blacked out.
Without alcohol.
I was a bag of nerves.
This all meant something, I was sure, but what it meant escaped me.

Before rock was a confusing mish-mash of bad relationships and stumbling around a vegan deli, trying to figure out what I was going to do with my life. It was like I lived inside a Goya painting, was a brilliant stroke of a Caravaggio. I was so deeply drawn to the expressions of dead people. People from long ago. I could feel them. Safe people. Dead people. Intimacy was such a challenge. In order for me to feel anything on a deep level, it had to be dead.

I constantly digressed.

Sigh.

Trevor changed all that. Trevor was alive. All heartbeat and muscle, twinkle, life, smile, sex god. Trevor was right now. The past and future, yes, but definitely right now. I wanted to lean over and kiss him again, but that wasn't fair to Dylan. Dylan had the awkward privilege of being my best friend as well as Trevor's best friend. An odd threesome on a crucifix built for two.

I was busy nailing myself to crosses for the ridiculous choices I'd made, but I wasn't alone. Trevor was backtracking in an effort to move forward. I was being driven out to see a psychic at 2 AM because nothing screams fucked up like blacking out with a glowing alien rock in your hands, standing in a hole in the desert with unidentified lights flashing overhead.

Oh, and your ex-boyfriend is there.

Married to someone else.

And you realize you should have never, ever left him.

Because.

He's the man of your dreams.

Except—

You haven't had that dream yet.

And that bothers you.

Because, how in the world are you supposed to know it's love?

Real. True. Love.

Trevor leaned into me and I inhaled deep. A lifetime of melting into him was all I wanted. Ten lifetimes. Twenty. A hundred billion lifetimes.

And one moment of clarity.

Just one.

One dazzling moment of incredible clarity where I knew I was finally making the right decision.

A single sign from the universe.

Out of the corner of my eye in the dashboard light, Dylan reached forward and turned the knob on the radio. Static crackled. A jumbled bunch of voices and songs collided as his fingers turned the knob.

Then I heard, "Just the two of us. We can make it if we try. Just the two of us, building castles in the sky. Just the two of us."

Trevor squeezed my thigh and sang, "You and I."

Two.

One more than one.

You and me.

My parents loved that song. Now they were back in the desert, where we could have tea parties and Stella could cover the lazy cat with sand in the sandbox.

I sighed, and Trevor squeezed my hand.

My childhood was over.

My teens were over.

And yet, my parents were back.

As brightly in love as ever.

Perfect role models.

Yet there I was, squeezed into the front seat of a twenty-year-old pickup truck, wondering if I could ever love the man I was so obviously in love with.

André was in the front parlor when the three of us wandered in. From the side window, I could see the pink rock glow under the tarp.

Dylan lifted a business card from the table. "I've driven past this place for years."

André squeezed his palms together. "Well, now you're an insider."

Trevor threw his arm over Dylan's shoulder. "How does it feel?"

Running his hand over the top of the velvet loveseat, Dylan said, "It feels good."

Pleased, André nodded. "Then make yourself at home. Skye and I will be out in a minute."

As soon as we were in the back room, André closed the door and whispered, "Have you been lighting the candles?"

Making excuses to a psychic was an all-time low. "I'm not really good with schedules, and today was exceptionally weird."

Pulling a chair back from the table, he gestured for me to take a seat. "How so?"

Taking a deep breath, I took a leap, letting go of the few remaining shreds of my sanity. "Because my sister had to go to the courthouse, and there was this phantom dog, and I was out in the desert pulling a weird, pink rock out, and then all of a sudden there were lights above my head, and I think I blacked out, and then my parents came back to town."

He leaned across the table, "You saw the lights?"

What I really liked about André was that out of everything I'd just said, the only part that struck him as odd were the lights.

"Yes. It was the second time."

His mouth fell open. "That's a good sign."

"You know what I'm talking about?"

Laying his hands flat on the table, he was quiet, in a dramatic pause sort of way. "I've seen the lights before."

Caught off guard, I leaned closer. "What do they mean?"

André raised an eyebrow and shrugged. "I'm trying to figure out the same thing. A guy I've been seeing gives me coordinates when the lights appear on radar."

That caught me off guard. "Aaron's gay?"

Surprising a psychic is no small task.

André cocked his head, brow pinched tight. "You know Aaron?"

"He's Trevor's cousin."

"Who's Trevor?"

Nodding in the direction of the lobby, I said, "Daisy Dukes and mohawk."

André exhaled. "You know he figures greatly into your future, right?"

The sudden shifts in topic were jarring. My day was complicated enough. I nodded slowly.

"Why the hesitation?"

"It's a little bumpy right now."

André leaned back, regarding me a moment. "Fair enough. I want you to do something."

Gah. More homework.

"I want you to practice Ho'oponopono."

"Ho-opono*what?*"

"When I was learning how to use my gift, I went to a small island in Hawaii where a Kahuna taught me the practice. It's like a way to clear the space and forgive ourselves. People think forgiveness is about other people. Forgiveness is about us and for us. If you can't forgive yourself, you get stuck. You think you made a mistake. Really, you just made choices."

"Okay," I swallowed, not sure if I should board the Ho ship yet.

"We're only broken if we can't see how whole we are."

Tears pushed against my eyelids. "You mean me?"

"I mean anyone."

"What do I do?"

"Light a candle. Say a prayer. Ho'oponopono is technically a fourteen-step process, but it clears your old karma. I want you to find a quiet place and say, 'I'm sorry. Forgive me. Thank you. I love you.' When you forgive yourself, your light will shine."

"Is that what the rock is trying to teach me?"

"Well, I never even thought about that. Maybe."

"How do I get back to who I was?"

"You don't need to get back to who you were. You just need to be in charge of who you are now."

I smiled, nervous, not in charge. "Is this a New Age pep talk?"

André stood, touching my hand gently. "I'm sorry. Forgive me. Thank you. I love you."

A quiet calm swept over me. It was a jarring, odd sense,; all that calm.

"Has anything else happened?"

I told him about the beetles.

"Hmm," he lowered himself back into his chair. "Beetles relate to threes. Three very important events will occur."

"Can you see what they are?"

"I can see that your choices have a hand in this."

"My choices have a hand in everything. That's how I ended up in this confusing mess where the past and future intersect, jamming me in the middle."

"Well, beetles come to people who struggle with being honest. A metamorphosis is coming to your life. Be ready, Skye. This is big."

Chills ran down my forearms, and suddenly the small room felt large and spacious. I inhaled deep. *Bugs mean big.*

André stood again. "Remember, light a candle. Say a prayer. Ho'oponopono."

Trevor and Dylan were on the front porch playing fight club. Not the brawling, sweating, face-pounding from the movie, but the kind where they punched each other in the shoulder until one of them squealed like a bitch, thereby declaring a winner.

"Why didn't anyone mention Aaron is gay?"

Trevor stopped and raised an eyebrow. "He flies it under the radar because of his job."

"Well, it's not like I walk around announcing my sexual orientation, but it would have been nice to know."

"You can announce your sexual orientation later," Trevor said with a smirk.

I rolled my eyes, but it was one of the first flirty things he'd said since I'd gotten back. "I'll take you up on that."

"Looking forward to it."

Dylan cleared his throat and plopped down on the edge of the porch. "So, what happened in there?"

I shrugged. "He held my hand and said the beetles represent three events."

"Did he charge you for that?"

"No. The hand touching was totally free."

Trevor looked out to the endless black sky rolling away. "I don't know how I feel about that."

"Not charging me?"

"Touching you."

"It was harmless. What you will find interesting is that he's seen the lights."

Without hesitation, Trevor spun around to face me. "Introduce us."

"I just—he's closed."

Walking to the front door, he said, "Come on, Skye. Just do it. I've never asked anything of you. Please do this one thing."

I looked to Dylan for help, but all he did was shrug and say, "He asked nicely."

Trevor was a personality of extremes. All in or all out. Never a man to waffle once a decision had been made.

I knew he wouldn't let it go. He'd pitch a tent on the front porch to prove a point.

I knocked softly, hoping André wouldn't hear me.

A few seconds later, I heard the clack of heels, and the door opened. "Did you forget something?"

I gestured to Trevor. The thing about Trevor was that he's a big dude. Broad chest and wide shoulders. All legs and arms and torso, with a mohawk standing straight up on the top of his head. That, combined with an impressive resting bitch face, made him a fairly intimidating mortal.

"Skye said you saw the lights out in the desert."

André's shoulders relaxed. "Yeah. Why?"

"What do you think they are?"

Leaning against the door frame, André gave it some thought. After all, it was 3 AM in the middle of nowhere. Real crazy takes time to cultivate.

"I'll tell you what I know," he said, "if it shows up on radar, then it's not flashing lights from carnivals or casinos."

"I think it knows who we are," Dylan said from the side of the porch.

André's eyes flashed bright.

"Yes. Like it's trying to tell us something. Or show us something."

"How many times have you seen it?" Trevor asked.

"Twice. But I work mostly in the evenings, so I don't come outside a lot. How many times have you seen it?"

"Five," Trevor said.

"Six," Dylan raised his hand.

André turned to me. "You?"

"Twice. The first time I had very vivid memories from my childhood. The second time, I just sorta blanked."

"Aaron said there is absolutely no way this is military craft," Trevor added.

"How is any of this even possible," I wondered.

"Because there's something beyond all this," Dylan said.

André inhaled sharply and yawned. "Apologies. That wasn't in response to the company."

"I get it," I said. "This has been one of the longest days of my life. We'll report back if we see something."

André turned to Trevor. "It was nice to meet you. We'll see each other again, I'm sure. Small town."

Trevor shook hands with him. "Also, you're dating my cousin."

André actually blushed in the porch light. "There's that."

Dylan drifted in from the edge and shook hands.

I was down the steps on the brick walk when André said, "Wait."

I stopped and turned around.

"Does the word 'monkey' mean anything?"

My entire body shivered all at once. A violent tremor, like cold metal surging through my veins. I didn't have to turn around to see the shock on Trevor's face. I could feel it.

Standing with his back to me, I heard Trevor swallow and say, "It means something to me. Why?"

"Did you have a monkey as a child?"

"It was my nickname. Because I climbed everything. T-monkey."

André's eyes drifted to the porch ceiling like he was listening. Moments passed. Quiet moments, where everyone breathed deeper, waiting.

Finally, André dropped his chin. "Your mother wants you to know how much she loves you. She said to tell you that when the hurt comes, follow it with forgiveness. Forgiveness is the path forward." Then he turned to Dylan, "She said to tell you 'kowabunga'."

I'd never seen Trevor cry. In nine years, I'd never even seen him misty-eyed. He was a champion at expressing his emotions, but he didn't linger. Not like me. Tender, yes. Tears, never.

"Tell her I love her," Trevor whispered.

André inhaled, closing his eyes. "She can feel it."

"It still feels good to say it."

André exhaled into the desert night. "Yes. Yes, it does."

Trevor looked down the steps, and I held out my hand.

Stifling another yawn, André said, "I'll be in touch."

With that he was gone, closing the door behind him softly.

Stars blazed in the night, pulsing, alive. Vibrant bursts of light and energy. Maybe my life had unfolded in a maze of confusion and chaos. But, standing on that porch, all of us, at that moment, meant something.

I was sure of it.

Letting my eyes drift to that brilliant sky, I wondered aloud, "Why do you think we can't get to other worlds?"

Dylan jumped down, avoiding the stairs. "Because people love their pain."

Pink light seeped from under the edges of the tarp.

Trevor stared right at Dylan. "Sometimes you slay it with one sentence, dude. *One sentence.* You need your own YouTube channel."

Dylan winked. "Pythagoras got along just fine without the internet."

CHAPTER THIRTEEN

My parents were night owls. Part of the allure of RV life was eat when hungry, sleep when tired. In high school, it was fun to have them up in the middle of the night, because it meant I could be up, too. But walking into Stella's kitchen at 4:06 AM to find Daddy in mid-scoop made me anxious. There was a dead chinchilla in the freezer. Explaining that to my sister had been awkward enough.

"Hey, Mr. D.," Trevor said without so much as a flinch.

"Daddy," I said, "What are you doing?"

"Making some cheap decaf I found in the cabinet."

Daddy shook hands with Trevor, organized crime cryptic code, finger grasp. "Drink?"

"Sure," Trevor said, "I could use one. Maybe not coffee, though. A beer?"

I could use a drink. I could use a month of drinks, and a life coach, and someone to work out all the details of my life that had eluded me so far. Like Oprah, if she were a drill sergeant and a preacher, but bigger, meaner looking, someone who swore like Gordon Ramsey and didn't take anyone's whiny shit, like Dr. Phil. Or Thor.

Mom was in the living room texting.

"Hey," I said. "You guys are up late."

She looked up from her phone and smiled so bright I actually melted. My mother, *the charmer.*

"We're always up late."

"What are you doing?"

"Talking to a friend."

"At 4 AM?"

"The ones you can talk to at 4 AM are the only ones that count. But seriously," she said, finishing up and setting her phone on the coffee table, "our friends are like us. They stay up late. We took a detour to come back here and see everyone. Our friends are nosy and curious. They worry about us"

That made me jealous, if I was being honest.

Which wasn't my strength, *honestly.*

I was very good at being contrary and paradoxical. My sister and I were once their entire world. I'd commanded everyone's focus. The intensity of those hard-won stares made me nervous, or stupid, or *something*. I'd turned away, and they'd cast their gaze in other directions, and then I felt alone. A stupid, irresponsible cycle. A selfish cycle of, 'Look at me! Look at me!' Then, 'Go away. I don't need you.' A childish cycle. My cycle. My spinning, ridiculous, dizzying descent into a placid unhappiness that had overtaken my life.

"Skye?"

I looked up from where I'd been staring, at her phone next to the untended Zen garden. "Yes?"

"Are you okay?"

I nodded fakely and said, "Of course." Shaking off my self-centered reflections, I stayed in character and lied. "Just a little tired."

"Oh, I know," she gushed. "Adam and I stay up so late that we forget other people have schedules."

My dad. Adam. The first man. It was so weird to hear someone call him by his first name. To me he was Daddy. *My daddy.*

Trevor walked in sipping a beer in a plain water glass, because my sister bought all her dishes at the dollar store. "Hey, Mrs. D."

My mom gave me the side eye, and smirked. She'd always liked Trevor. "Marry the man who makes your heart sing, and your whole life will be a song," she whispered.

So far, I hadn't been so good with that advice. Maybe I'd thought that if the guy could sing, then there would be song even if I wasn't feeling it. Maybe the chords would play themselves until I caught on. Some weird logic lost in translation. A harmony I couldn't quite ease into.

Daddy threw his arm around my shoulder and handed me a beer. "For you," he said. "To celebrate your return."

Re-turn.

Like I'd turned.

Then turned back.

"Sit down," Mom said.

We all sat. Mom in the chair next to Dad, holding hands. Me and Trevor on the sofa, awkwardly staring at my parents like I was sixteen all over again, with Daddy pointing at the shotgun he used to keep loaded next to the front door, explaining how he liked for his daughter to be home on time.

"So, what have you been up to?" Daddy asked Trevor.

Leaning back, Trevor let his drink rest on his knee. "Working at Golden Years."

"You're a caregiver?" Mom asked.

"Maybe not so much a caregiver as a heavy lifter. I pretty much float around all day and help the clients in and out of beds and showers."

"You see old people naked?" Mom asked, stuck on this line of questioning.

"All the time."

"Is that weird?"

"Nah, we have these big towels and I help them in and out of their shower chairs. Only Mrs. Finglestein flashes me a little boob every now and then."

"So, what are your plans," Daddy asked, like we had any.

"I've got a few ideas I've been kicking around. I'm still incubating."

I should have been interested in his plans for the future, but all I could think about was how good Trevor smelled. Sweat and cologne and dreamy hotness. I wondered if he'd let me climb onto his lap in my bedroom and touch myself while I rubbed my titties all over his bare chest, like I had some sexual compulsive disorder.

"Sounds like a plan," Daddy said. "Don't you think, Skye?"

"Huh? What?"

"Trevor," Mom pointed, "going into business for himself."

I looked over and smiled. A flashing, wayward smile I hoped distracted everyone from the fact that I had my own personal porno playing in my head. Trevor squeezed my knee. I sipped my beer and leaned closer. I was, after all, sitting in a room with my parents and my high school crush.

"Well, it's good to see everyone back together again," Daddy said. "Where's Dylan?"

"He had this rock thing to take care of."

"A rock thing?" Mom asked.

"A rock," Trevor clarified. "He had to take it home."

"He was always rather unique," Dad said, finishing off his decaf. "Well, I will let you two get some sleep. Willa and I are going out to look at the stars."

Named after Willa Cather, because that was my grandmother's favorite writer.

Death Comes for the Archbishop.

The Song of the Lark.

Shadows on the Rock.

One of Ours.

"I wanted to walk straight on through the red grass and over the edge of the world, which could not be very far away."

I might be brushing up on my London, but I knew my Willa Cather. Back when I was twelve it was a cool line. Later, it sorta highlighted my impulsive, odd behavior. In that moment, it made me realize in a terrifying, come-to-Jesus moment that maybe I'd spent years walking close to the edge only because it was safe. Not cool or edgy, but safe. From that edge, I'd built a wall so I neither had to go inland nor over into the abyss, down to the flat bottom of the canyon where the coyote went *splat*. I could just stay right there, forever. Thinking. Overthinking. Rethinking. *God, I thought a lot.*

Mom walked over and hugged me at an awkward angle. "I love looking up. That's why I named you Skye."

My parents, with all their flirting and loving touches, which embarrassed me to no end when I was in school, could still slay me with a sentence.

My grandmother Tula always said, "Don't worry about being a girl. Worry about who you are and what you're doing in this world." It was like I'd come from this long line of strong, amazing women, and stalled.

The strong had gone to Stella.

Mom squeezed me tight.

I inhaled her perfume. A new one I'd never smelled before. Strawberries and vanilla, with a sharper scent like bourbon in the base. A lovely gourmand fragrance. "I love you," I said. I thought I'd burst into tears if I said anything else. Also, I wondered constantly where she'd made a turn, a real definitive turn in life, and I'd just gotten lost.

Daddy squeezed me into a bear hug. "I'm so glad we're all back together."

Which was odd, coming from a man who ran off with his wife literally days after I graduated high school.

I nodded. "I know."

It was true. For as disturbing as it was to have to sit on a sofa facing my parents with my high school crush at my side, it was tremendous relief. Or surrender. Maybe abandon.

In all the meditation I'd done in South Carolina, the one thing I'd been terrible about was letting go.

Let it go, Skye.

Let go.

It was like the hardest thing in the world. Hanging from the monkey bars of life, I squeezed so tight I couldn't breathe.

Let go, Skye.

Daddy backed up and regarded me a moment. "Are you happy to be back?"

The time for honesty had come. "Kind of. I have mixed feelings."

"Fair enough."

Mom giggled behind him. "Come on, Adam."

Adam and Willa, sitting in a tree.

"You'll come through this, baby Skye," he said, squeezing my shoulders, looking a little worried.

As soon as the kitchen door closed, I sighed.

"It's late," Trevor said softly. "Mind if I crash here?"

Crash into me. The Dave Matthews of my childhood. I'm the king of the castle. You're the dirty rascal. Crash into me. All of our atoms colliding in the superconductor of life. Maybe instead of totally obliterating each other, we transform into some fourth dimensional creation that lives on the edge of a star being born.

"Sure," I said, "follow me." The words coming out of my mouth formed in the early dawn, and I was certain that's what I'd been saying to Trevor all along. *Follow me.* The trouble was, I had absolutely no idea where I was going.

You know that feeling you have when you meet someone, and you want to stay up all night smoking cigarettes, sitting across from each other in a booth, drinking coffee? *Yeah*, I'd always had that feeling with Trevor. As soon as my head hit the pillow, I was wide awake in an exhausted euphoria that bled from my pores. Laying on the bed in my sister's guestroom, I was tempted to do all sorts of things. Being so close to him made me crazy.

Staring at shadows on the ceiling, he asked, "Where do we go from here?"

"Away."

"You already tried that, Skye."

I sighed in the cool blue light of dawn. "Maybe we start over."

"Are we starting over or just starting? It always felt like we were in limbo before, and when our feet finally touched the ground, you took off."

My entire world spun upside down, making me dizzy. It was such a blindingly obvious statement, gifted with a staggering amount of truth. A sharp, raw, clear moment.

I closed my eyes in the dark, imagining that, if I laid perfectly still and listened, I could hear the sound of the end coming. Like a sharp chapter break. Like every sound pushing forward. Tracks winding into a new future. One I couldn't see, because I was still stuck in the backseat of my past life. It felt like I'd been riding shotgun my whole life. I was ready to climb into the driver's seat and put my foot on the gas. Paradoxically, I felt like I'd driven the same roads too fast and too long. Maybe I just needed to accept that everything before was preparation. Like I'd been fixing my hair for a decade. Like I'd learned to drink the poison slowly to build up an immunity.

Like one ray of light cracking through all that dark matter. And by dark matter, I meant the intimate layers of my life. And by intimate layers, I meant the bullshit I obsessed over.

I wanted to stab my eyeballs out with the sharp indecision that ruled my life. A never-ending loop of *oh my God what do I do next*. A never-ending loop where time and change were dressed all in black and hid in the shadows, and I could never get my hands on them. Laying in the dark, I considered many options, but chose the unthinkable one. Before I could talk myself out of it, before I could compile a whole list in my head of why I shouldn't do it, I rolled over swiftly in bed, straight on top of Trevor's broad, handsome chest.

"Whoa, hey, Skye," Trevor said, reaching for my hips and holding on. "I thought you said you're tired?"

"Well, here's the thing: I think I've said a lot of things that don't really line up with what I want. So, I am taking this opportunity to change."

"I accept," he said. In the faint light coming through the window, I saw him smile. Then, his mouth was on mine, and all the thoughts in my head disappeared.

Okay, that's not true, because you've been listening to this story for a while now, and I wasn't really capable of erasing all the thoughts whizzing through the asylum called my mind. Still, it was close. I loved the feeling of Trevor's mouth on mine. The lush kiss. I loved how he kissed me like it was the first and last time *every time.* I loved feeling my body lying on top of him. How he made me feel like this tiny girl laying on his huge body. In Trevor's hands, I could do anything. Fly to Mars. Hold back tsunamis with my bare hands. Trevor made me feel strong and delicate, beautiful and fierce.

If I could get my brain to shut up.

He wrapped his arms around me and squeezed my ass, and I slid my hands under his shirt, feeling the smooth skin of his chest, the rough hairs against my fingertips. Trevor was the single most luscious thing I'd ever known.

Pushing my hands up, I lifted his shirt and buried my face in his chest, licking his nipples, breathing in the scent of his skin.

I melted like a pool of warm butter on organic, gluten-free toast. Squeezing him tight in-between my legs, I raised my face and went back for the kiss. The long, perfect kiss, so turned on, it felt like I was floating. Suddenly, my entire existence was a warm kiss. I pushed his shirt up farther, and he raised his arms over his head so I could pull it off. It had been so long since I'd undressed Trevor, I forgot how sexual it was to see his head pop out of the opening of his shirt and see the broad expanse of his chest naked in the dim light. The sight made me quiver. I squeezed him with my thighs to hold myself upright. I was about to swoop down and have the hottest make-out session in my entire life when I heard a tiny *clank*. Then I was blinded by a bright light. Right in my face. Like the bright light at the end of the tunnel when you die.

"What the fuck?" I heard Trevor say, but I couldn't see. He rolled me off and jumped out of bed, hitting his knee on the nightstand, then half-limped, half-stumbled to the window where I knew the blinds were open, because I constantly forgot to close them at night.

"What's going on out there?" I asked, squeezing my eyes shut to make the ache stop.

Trevor bent the blinds and I rolled out of bed, feeling my way to the window.

"It's just the flood lights. One of them is turned at an angle so it shines right into your room."

Out on the lawn, perfectly illuminated, my parents played croquette. A weird Alice in Wonderland in the low desert. Daddy was bent over, a cigar gripped between his teeth. Mom laughed, pointing her mallet straight up at the sky full of stars. Daddy whacked the croquet ball, and it rolled across the sandy, pebbled yard. My whole body deflated. I wanted to celebrate the fact they were up in the middle of the night playing croquet, laughing under the stars but, as it turned out, I was a selfish asshole who couldn't just shut up and order the fish.

Trevor sighed. "Looks like your dad turned on the floodlights so they can play that Alice in Wonderland game in the front yard."

"Croquet."

"I beg your pardon?"

"It's called croquet. And Daddy loves it."

"By the looks of it, so does your mom."

My turn to sigh. "She loves her life."

Trevor turned me around in his arms. "You say that like it's a bad thing."

I let my body ease into his. "I say it because it's true, and I don't know what that feels like."

His hands moved to my back. At first it tickled, then it was weird. "What's going on?" I giggled.

"I lost my bracelet," he said, stepping back. "The one my mom gave me when I graduated."

"Check under the bed. I thought I heard something fall."

Trevor launched himself onto the small bed and thrust his hand down between the mattress and the wall. After a second, he said, "The bed is too close to the wall. My arm won't fit."

I flipped on the bedside lamp and got down on my hands and knees. Feeling around in the dark, my fingers touched metal. I was just about to pull it out when I saw mine and Trevor's initials written in permanent marker on the bed frame.

I pushed backwards and stared.

Trevor furrowed his brow and swung around. After a second, his brow smoothed and raised. Then, he actually laughed. "This is your old bed from high school, Skye. Did you know that?"

I fell back on my heels and huffed. "No. I did not. I assumed when my parents sold their house and went to live in the RV that they sold the furniture."

"Looks like they gave it to your sister instead."

"Thank you, Captain Obvious."

"So, here we are, laying in the bed where I first took your panties off."

I stood up and twisted the blinds closed.

Trevor laid back on his elbows. "You don't want to be reminded of the first time I took your panties off?"

"I don't want to be reminded that we are in my childhood bed."

"You weren't exactly a child."

I spun around to find him reclined, smiling, pleased with himself.

"You, me, and Dylan are such children we should be living in a tree house."

Trevor pursed his lips and thought for a second. "Okay, I accept. We can all go live in a tree house together, but Dylan gets his own branch 'cause he's kind of a slob."

I put my hands on my hips because I wasn't going to allow silly to derail my serious moment.

Trevor stretched his arms over his head, letting his legs fall open. "Wrapping this back around to my original point," he said, "I'd like to take your panties off in our tree house."

Admissions like the one above stopped me in my tracks. *Every. Single. Time.* It's like a drug. An overwhelming, delicious, orgasmic drug. Trevor Drug. I wanted a box of Trevor. You know, the kind that is ready to eat when you open it. A box of frosted Trevor. A carton of him, with extra pulp, because nothing—and I do mean nothing—tastes as good as a tall glass of fresh-squeezed Trevor. Canned Trevor in heavy syrup, because someday I will open it in an emergency. Chocolate-covered Trevor to melt on my tongue, and Trevor berries to whip into a frenzy with yogurt and cream. Trevor beans, because they come in all flavors, and I love Trevorine. Maybe a little Tex-Mex Trevor smothered in hot hot hot sauce, and one sweet gooey bar of caramel-covered Trevor, and one case of diet Trevor, because the bubbles tickle my nose. Instant Trevor, poached Trevor, and Trevor Trevor Trevor Trevor until my brain explodes.

"Skye?" Trevor whispered.

I glanced down at him. "Yes?"

"Are you okay?"

"I was, ummm… thinking about a prayer André told me to recite."

"That's odd."

Trying to get out of my awkward neurosis, I nodded and said, "Let me get your bracelet," because I was in bed with my ex-boyfriend from high school while my parents played croquet under the stars.

CHAPTER FOURTEEN

I woke at 1:06 PM to the sound of knocking on my window. For a brief second, I lay there, hoping Trevor would roll over and kiss me. When I sat up and realized he was gone with a note folded on his pillow, I could live with that.

The glass rattled as someone banged from outside. Walking down the dim hall, I read the quick note, which turned out to be a scribble of extremely romantic poetry.

e. e. cummings.

{swoon}

I opened the door and looked out into the carport to see my Mom bent over, wearing a pair of pink pedal pushers, trying to see into my bedroom window.

"Nosy," I said.

Snapping upright, she smiled when she saw me. "Forgetful. I accidentally left the keys Stella gave us on the kitchen counter and locked myself out." The beetles skittered to and fro.

Glancing over, I saw the key chain and remembered, somewhat strangely, that I hadn't seen my sister in a while. She'd been like that since we were kids, coming and going, the flow of Stella leaving a trail of dirty socks and underwear behind.

"Whew, it's hot." Mom stepped into the kitchen and closed the door.

The room dimmed considerably with the door shut.

"I was making your father and I a pot of coffee this morning and saw Trevor leave." She nudged me that way girls do when they are impressed.

Unwilling to lead her on, I said, "He was too tired to drive."

Mom winked at me. "Okay, you tell that lie however you need to."

"That's not fair."

"Are my comments supposed to be fair?"

"Well, one of your daughters is a corrections officer. I would think you know something about fairness."

Mom leaned in and whispered, "The truth is, I've never really understood your sister's career choice."

"Stella is an ass kicker."

"Well, yes," she conceded.

"When she dies, she's going to be a bouncer at the gates of heaven."

Mom's eyes drifted to the ceiling as she considered this a moment. "Noble and lofty. I like it. Why don't you let me buy you lunch, baby Skye?"

Mom and dad are the only ones who called me Baby Skye. Next to Trevor, it was my second drug of choice. Like in middle school, when we crushed up SweeTarts on our desk and snorted them, because the substitute teacher always went to the teachers' lounge to smoke. We knew it was dumb, but someone told us sugar entered our bloodstream faster through our nose, so we did it against better judgement. Because, why in the world would anyone want good judgement in middle school? It ruined the entire experience.

While I've always been weird about my food, I've never liked the amount of utter arrogance that comes with eating healthy. With that in mind, we ended up at my mother's favorite spot. She loved a good dive.

The Bunker delivered in spades.

A diner started by a family of eight who lived in a camper down by the border. They worked construction out of that camper and saved their money. About a decade ago, they bought the old diner. The two youngest had gone to school with me and Dylan and Trevor. Apparently, they'd pooled their money together in a one-gallon jar until, one day, they bought the old Hershel Diner and changed the name to their name. Bunker.

Linoleum. Grease. Plastic booths in primary colors. A person's arteries trembled just driving by the place. A server with the nametag *Phatt G* had an armload of plastic baskets lined with white-and-red-checkered wax paper. Grilled cheese. Chili cheese dog. French fries smashed and dashed, jalapenos and melted cheese, onions, and barbeque on top of fries, one hamburger, two large hush puppies, cornbread made from real corn, and a side of chili to crumble it on.

I'd gotten used to the tiny portions served in my favorite restaurants, but my stomach had not. I stuffed my face with one bite after another. Cornbread, chili, grilled cheese, fries. I was going to eat my angst.

For years I'd been overwhelmingly, ravenously hungry.

Dad had a soft spot for sweets. Mom had a soft spot for anything deep fried. The hush puppy was as big as her fist.

"Some things change. Some things don't," she said, letting her eyes sweep over the yellowed ceiling. "It keeps the balance."

And that exchange will tell you everything you need to know about my mom. A modern-day Zen master in her pedal-pushers and Michael Kors bag, who could take down an entire army with a shotgun and a boomerang. She'd always been like that. Fearless and bold and beautiful. Like, Stella.

I actually sighed.

I hadn't even bothered to brush my hair before I put it in a ponytail. I could never compete with my mom's pure beauty.

She raised an eyebrow. "How is Trevor?"

"Are you asking because you want to know if love is in the air?"

Laughing, she wiped her ketchup-stained fingers on a paper napkin and said, "I know love is in the air. I've seen the way he looks at you."

"And how is that?"

"Like a man who gets a second chance to grab the one thing he knows is precious."

"I'm hardly precious, Mom."

"You're all hard rock and crackle paint on the outside, but you're a love bunny inside."

Love bunny.

Baby Skye.

Let me drown in silly baby talk.

We could curl up and read Little House on the Prairie. The entire set. With Ma and Pa on the prairie, with the dog, and wagons, and horses, and absolutely no resemblance to my current reality.

It took me mere seconds to regress.

"And how do I look at him," I asked, before sinking my teeth into a chili cheese dog, mustard, relish, onions, and sauerkraut.

"Like a girl who knows it was love at first sight but wants a second opinion."

"Slick observation."

Her hand fluttered in the air, and the light flashed across the wedding ring Daddy designed. Moonstone with Citrine. Glitter nail polish. My mother, style icon.

"I have my moments."

More like lifetimes. My mom put moments on the map. She was the only person, other than Daddy, who took the brightest and best moments and made them shine brighter. It was her superpower. One of them, at least.

She knew how to shine.

She shined so much, she glowed.

"What about you? Are you going to stay here and have some moments, or are you going to be a gypsy like me and your father?"

"Are you asking me if I'm going to marry Trevor?"

"I know you're going to marry Trevor. I've known it since you were sixteen and went on your first date and came home all moony-eyed."

Flamethrower of snark incoming. "You know he married someone else, right?"

"What I am asking is: what are you going to do with your life?"

"Do I have to answer that right away, or can I review my notes and get back to you after I smother my problems in grease and watch them slide away?"

Because boy, had I ever compiled some notes on life. None of them made sense, but I had a vault full of useless observations stuffed deep in the pit of my brain.

Lesson number one: you literally have no fucking clue what is going to happen in life.

Finishing off a hush puppy, she laughed. "Have you gone back to see the old house?"

The very thought was jarring. "No. Why would I do that?"

Mom furrowed her pretty brow. "Because it's nice to sometimes see where you've been. Where we were as a family. Where we are now. We had some really good times in that house."

"Which doesn't explain why you sold it," I jabbed.

The pretty furrow turned to an outright scowl. "You can't run off and then be upset when people make decisions without you."

"I just don't understand why you had to sell it. You could have rented it out."

"And be landlords on the road?"

"Sure," I shrugged.

"You're just being difficult. Your father and I are doing something totally different and really enjoying ourselves. Traveling is a lot of work. We don't want the added work of owning a house."

"So, you're just going to drive around your whole lives."

That little piece of sarcasm got me the eyebrow lift. "We're not driving. We're living. You should try it."

For the first time in my life, my mom totally dissed me, in public, with a French fry in her hand.

It was so fucking dignified I could cry.

I heard Stella behind me. "Skye, is that you?"

I turned around. I'd never been so glad to see my redneck sister in all my life.

"What are you doing here," I asked, but she didn't have to answer, because two seconds later Dylan walked through the door, making the little bell jingle.

"You just saved me from the *what are you going to do with your life* question," I whispered to Dylan as he slid into the booth next to me.

"I can go back out to the car and wait if you'd like to think about your answer."

I shook my head.

"Hey, Mrs. D."

"How's the bull semen business going?"

I turned to him so fast I felt my brain slosh around in my head. "You told my mom about the bull semen?"

Shrugging, he grabbed a handful of fries. "It's not like it's a secret."

Changing the subject, I looked at Stella, "So, how are you?"

She shrugged. "Good. So, what are you going to do with your life?"

"You first."

"I might not understand the nature of reality," Stella said, "but I washed my car and bought a grill."

"Fuck yeah," Dylan held up his palm for a high-five that Stella promptly slapped.

That is how slackers encourage other slackers.

"I'm just worried about you. When you were little, you were so happy, and you misplaced that along the way," Mom said.

"Skye needs to learn how to be happy just sitting out in the front yard drinking a beer."

I wanted to stab my eyes out with the little plastic knife I used to cut my hot dog. "Stop talking about me like I'm not here."

Stella turned in her seat to face me. "It's not that you don't know what you want, it's that you want everything, and you want it to be perfect. Like, all the time. You're so afraid of things ending that you never begin. You've been doing this your entire life."

I pinched up my nose.

Dylan flagged down a server and ordered half the menu, smothered in cheese and extra barbeque. I took the opportunity to shift from what we were talking about to new and interesting things we *could* be talking about.

"Can you put cherries in my Coke," Dylan yelled after our server, who nodded without looking back.

"You liked fashion," Mom said.

"Guys, can we talk about something else?"

"Not to dicker, but there are way more girls at this table than guys," Stella pointed out.

I gave her the stink eye. "Okay, *girls*, can we talk about something else?"

Stella snorted and elbowed Mom in the side. A boney elbow to the ribs.

Dylan inhaled, swallowed, and raised his eyebrow. "Stella is onto something."

"Really? You're actually siding with her?" I asked, totally annoyed.

"Hear me out. It's where you and I differ. We have a lot in common, but I don't really have this idea how things are supposed to be. Hell, I guess if you're doing it right you don't know the outcome, because you never in your wildest dreams expected anything so awesome to happen. You get hung up in the *how's,* Skye. The how it happens, and how it looks, and how it turns out. How matters, but it's not everything. The why and how and what and all the other stuff that goes into moments and life experiences unfolding makes up the whole thing."

"Did you really just use the words 'life experience' with me?"

Rolling his eyes, he said, "Alright, Diogenes, you are a true cynic."

"Okay," Mom said. "Let's look at this a different way. Let's all talk about what we wanted to be growing up, and how that blossomed in our lives. I'll go first."

I'll go first is a cheap shot. It assumes everyone will follow.

"When I was little, growing up in Alaska, I wanted to live with polar bears and own a flower shop."

"Daddy is kind of like a polar bear."

Mom smiled. "He's better than a polar bear, because he doesn't eat baby seals."

"Good point."

Mom turned to Dylan. "What did you want to be?"

Without hesitation, Dylan said, "A dinosaur."

I laughed. Like a really loud laugh that made other customers stare. It was awesome to know someone so long and not know all the details. I liked how they trickled out over years, years going on a decade. I liked how we couldn't just stay up all night and blurt out our life stories. There was too much.

"Well, that is an interesting career path," Mom said.

Dylan smiled. "Likewise, polar bear colonizer."

"Stella?"

Stella pulled her lips to the side, like she did when she was really thinking. "If I'm being truthful, I wanted to write country music songs."

Dylan turned to her. "Seriously?"

"Don't make fun of me."

"I'm not. I think that's really cool. You know I play guitar, right?"

"I've heard it mentioned," Stella smiled. Everyone at the table collectively lifted their eyes and let them fall on me. No pressure. Whatsoever. *Like, none.*

I had to compete with a song writer, a polar bear wrangler, and a dinosaur.

"I have a book that helps you identify your life mission," Mom said, helpfully.

They have a book on everything. Books on how to repair watches and broken relationships, how to maximize your time, make friends, and save more money for travel. I know. I read them all in South Carolina. Which didn't really explain why I was bumming around in the desert, unemployed.

Stella shrugged. "Look, this is simple. Figure out what you want to do and go for it."

Everyone at the table shifted their eyes from me to Stella. In her finer moments, she was a badass redneck Jedi Master, rehashing motivational sayings from the 90's, but her superpower was making me feel stupid. Stella stated the obvious in ways that made the truth gruesome. Texas Chainsaw Truth.

"I'm serious. Stop staring at me like I'm a freak. You get so lost in the details that you don't even know there *is* a big picture."

"And what is the big picture of my life, oh wise Stella?"

"You're on the verge of getting everything you want."

"Based on what?"

"Based on the life you've lived right up to this moment."

"I don't see it."

"You never see it. That's why we're all here at The Bunker, trying to figure out what you're going to do with your life."

"Because your life depends so much on the choices I make?"
It was mean. It even sounded mean coming out.

While Stella was straight up tough, she also had the ability to care without giving a fuck. "Because it sucks to watch people struggle."

Open the Earth and let me fall to the center. She said the S-word. I loathed the S-word. Because the truth was, I felt like I'd been struggling since middle school. Things were sometimes easy, but I couldn't just let them be easy, or let go. I worried constantly. I worried that I worried too much.

A mammoth pile of chili cheese-smothered fries, hot dogs, and a double stack patty melt with pickles and mustard covered in extra barbeque arrived. Dylan slipped into his happy place with the first bite.

I could smother my struggles in pickles.

Mom reached for my hand and squeezed. "This was good."

Stella shrugged. "Whatever you need to tell yourself."

Dylan and I stood in the parking lot, watching my mom and sister drive away.

"What do you think my sister wants," I asked, tossing my paper napkin into a trash can.

Dylan clicked his tongue on the roof of his mouth like he was about to drop a profound Dylanism. "A four-wheel drive, and any guy but me."

I tapped the top of the can, multitasking my thoughts. "That's not true."

He raised an eyebrow. "Just because you don't understand how your sister can resist my universal charm doesn't mean it isn't true. Just because you come from the same parents doesn't mean you'll be the same. Look, you're always angling to make a connection. It's part of who you are. You like the spaces where similarities overlap. That's fine, but there are different ways to see the same picture. You're so uptight."

I tightened my grip.

Dylan strolled ahead to his truck. "See, just mentioning how uptight you are makes you uptight. It's part of who you are. All that magnificent uptightness. But look how different you and I are, or, hell, you and Trevor. You and I are so different."

"So, opposites attract?"

"No. That's greeting card psychological masturbation bullshit code for the fact that no one has a real clue as to what chemistry is. The world isn't about making a connection with the same connection. It's about risking a connection with that thing that that might totally fry your circuits."

For the third time in less than forty-eight hours, I glared.

"Look," he said, turning around, "You can stink eye me all you want, Skye. It's the truth. You're always stumbling around, reeling over the fact that everyone is so different than you, when you should be smoking from the center."

"Yeah, well, we can't all move out to the middle of nowhere and sell bull semen that magically appeared."

"It's true," he said calmly, "Some of us had to run off and draw our feelings."

"You're an asshole."

"I can feel your snark all the way across the parking lot, Skye."

"That is not snark. It's envy. I would like to be a dinosaur with you."

I could see his eyes shift to the side behind his aviators. "Yeah?"

"Yeah. Trevor would make a great T-Rex."

"And you?"

"I feel confident that I'd make an outstanding Brontosaurus. You?"

"Strictly Stegosaurus over here. You should come with me, Bronto girl."

"Where exactly are we going?"

"We got a date with destiny, babe."

"Don't call me babe."

"Sweetie."

"I'm definitely not a sweetie."

"Sugar."

I thought about it a second and, as much as I didn't want to admit it, I could live with Sugar.

"Sugar Skye Dino-licious," Dylan howled.

It made me smile.

"But seriously, we need to drop our cell phones in a microwave oven I have stored in my tool box."

"Why do you have a microwave in a tool box?"

"The time for questions is later."

Standing at the back of his ratty pick-up truck with the scratched and rusted bed, blinding sun, and all that space rushing away in every direction, space that would never be filled, I admit I looked upon the microwave with a raised eyebrow. It was one of those odd, dorm room, studio apartment models.

Dylan extended his hand, palm up. Still deciding whether or not I should argue such a weird request, I dug around in my purse until I found my phone.

There was a dancing heart text from Trevor. My whole body melted into *Trevor Tremble*.

"Come on, you can return messages later," Dylan said.

CHAPTER FIFTEEN

There were a few things I'd always liked about Aaron. First, he was named after Elvis. Not in an overt way, but in the subtle, middle name way. A way to impress people with your parents' blatant love of pop culture, mashed up with baby-making. Second, he was the kid who always took the dare. A fearless, blond-haired, blue-eyed little pistol who ran circles around all us older kids.

Three counties over, in a totally different town, Aaron sat in a booth at the very back of a roadside diner.

Friendship involves cliques and cryptic backstory, but we took that to a whole new level. We'd all known each other forever. Dylan motioned for me to slide in across from Aaron.

Dylan slapped palms with Aaron, who leaned forward and said, "It's good to see you, Skye."

"You, too." I meant that, but I also meant the next part. "So, I'm guessing we didn't drive all the way out here for a reunion."

"No, we did not," Aaron said. "And since I'm on a schedule, I'll get to the point. Look, if I divulge exactly what I know, then the military won't just strip me of my clearance, they'll toss me in the brig and never let me out. So, the information I pass to you can't be information at all. I have to figure out a way to weave what I know into a story and that story into a code."

He pulled an odd stack of papers from a bag. Newspaper clippings, images from magazines, old pages from books, ripped out, with certain phrases circled in pencil. He pushed it toward me. Dylan intercepted, and nobody protested as he flipped through the pages.

"I know the news makes it seem like doing whatever you want with classified information ain't no big thing, and maybe for politicians that's true, but for the rest of us out here with an Above Top-Secret clearance, that shit just doesn't fly. At all. If I send one email to you with coordinates of a sighting, then this Air Force boy goes to jail. These things are heavily compartmentalized. So, what I've come up with are a few riddles for you to solve, and one clear truth. While I am forbidden to share classified information with anyone, I can tell you that you are hot on the trail of something real."

Dylan looked up from a page ripped from a book. "Real, how?"

Aaron locked eyes with Dylan and paused a second before saying, "Real in every sense of the word. Look, the Phoenix lights were real, and they were not military. People try to debunk that theory, and there's tons of doubters, but what I know for certain is that those most assuredly weren't flares, and the military dispatched aircraft to follow the Phoenix lights. It goes without saying that they weren't just lights."

Dylan was crazy enough without affirmation from other people. While I was intrigued by what Aaron said, I wasn't sure how I felt about all of us supporting Dylan in his quest to explain pink, glowing rocks and flaming cars.

"Seen anything cool lately?" Dylan asked, off-handed.

"Yes, sir, I have," Aaron responded.

I knew it was code. That was confusing, because my whole life felt like a code. One long riddle from beginning to end, where I bumped around in the labyrinth of images before I finally admitted I was lost.

"Okay," Dylan said, "Look, I get it. You're risking your life and career and freedom to point us in the right direction. I appreciate that, but give me an idea what I'm looking for."

"These lights come and go at the same coordinates, almost like clockwork."

"I thought you said they're not lights."

"They're not. But if I tell you what the military calls them, I'm divulging top-secret information. So, for the sake of conversation, I'm calling them lights."

I leaned forward, brow pinched tight. "Are you saying there are portals?"

Aaron said, "Well, I can neither confirm nor deny that," while nodding his head up and down.

Watching him closely, Dylan said, "Okay, you're saying portal."

"I'm saying there's a lot we don't know. Look, I'm saying the laws of physics apply to us on this planet. A binary star system operates differently. Some things stay the same, some change. Learn to see the world with a new pair of eyes. Learn to bend time."

"I don't understand what you're saying."

Aaron turned to me. "Why are you here, Skye?"

"I don't know," I answered, feeling dumb as soon as the words left my mouth.

"Don't you want to know?"

"Why I came back to the desert?"

"Get rid of your linear timeline. Why are you here?"

"Because I can't manage to find my way in the rest of the world," I said honestly, to offset the lunacy of my last comment.

"We are here because something put us here."

"Like God?"

"Like intention," Dylan jumped in.

"Intention put us here?"

"Look, everything is a frequency, a kind of sound. This frequency didn't arise from nowhere. It came from somewhere. It is perhaps hundreds of trillions of years old. But that frequency, at least in this world, is directed by intention. You intended to be Skye, and so here you are, with all your molecules formed to represent what we call Skye."

"My life is complicated enough without all this introspection."

"Life is even more complicated when you have no idea what you're doing."

"Well, I suffer from that, too."

Dylan laughed, stretching his arms out to either side. "The search for the meaning of life."

"You're insane."

"Possibly. Or maybe I'm enlightened."

Aaron gave Dylan an exaggerated side eye. "I don't know about enlightenment, but I do know if you follow these clues, you'll experience some pretty trippy stuff."

Our sever exited the kitchen with a huge tray, headed in the direction of a nearby table.

"That's all I'm going to say for now," Aaron nodded.

"I thought you were still in your parents' basement, playing video games and eating junk food," I said, not really done with the conversation, but understanding why he didn't want to talk in front of strangers.

Dylan slipped the stack of papers onto the plastic seat.

Aaron laughed. "The space to study and make connections is a true luxury, and I really took advantage of that back then."

Dylan turned to Aaron, "Alright, boss. We'll follow your clues."

Reaching over his empty coffee cup, Aaron said, "André told me you two met, and that he likes you."

"I'm very likeable," I smiled, only slightly sarcastic.

Squeezing my hand, he said, "More than you know."

All I knew was that we drove around the desert, constantly eating, and experiencing strange things no one could explain. If food was the meaning of life, it was pretty obvious I'd been ordering off the wrong menu.

Aaron picked up a banana from a nearby table. "Do you know what this is?"

I raised my eyebrows. "A piece of fruit?"

"No. It's a total mystery."

Whatever Dylan had was contagious. "Okay."

"Bananas share fifty percent of the same DNA as humans. So, when you eat a banana, it's a little more cannibalistic than you'd imagine, but that isn't the weird part. The weird part is that bananas don't seed. We're down here arguing about politics, when we really should be asking where the banana tree seed came from."

"You know the official story will be that a meteorite landed with a banana tree on it." Dylan rolled his eyes.

"That's fine. It still means somewhere in this vast universe, there is another planet with banana trees. We take these things for granted, but start asking yourself: where did the seed for a tree that doesn't seed come from?"

I smiled really big.

"Yeah, it's a nice thought, isn't it?"

"What if the tree of life is really a tree?" I asked.

Dylan turned to me, beaming, suddenly proud. "A tree. A seed. Oh my God, I've never thought about that."

"A tree needs water and light. Keep moving toward the light," Aaron said. Then he adjusted his aviators and walked out the door.

Dylan folded up his small stack of papers, stuffing them down the front of his jeans. "Man, I love that guy."

CHAPTER SIXTEEN

Dylan pulled into Stella's driveway. A huge box sat on her tiny front porch. It wasn't really a porch. More like a square of concrete with a faded roof.

The box read: *Fragile. Live. This Side Up.*

Dylan rammed the gearshift into park. "Did you order a puppy?"

I rolled my eyes. "I didn't order anything. I'm trying to make my last ten dollars stretch into the new year. Maybe Stella ordered something online and forgot to tell me."

"Well, I'm intrigued," Dylan announced, shoving his door open. "I'll race you," he yelled, but by the time I swung a leg out, he was already on the front porch, hunched over, reading the address. After a second he looked up, wearing the same expression as a dog who accidentally stepped in its own shit. "It's for you," he yelled.

After slamming the door three times to get it to latch, I walked over. "Who is it from?"

"I don't know," he said. "It's a company I've never heard of before."

"But I didn't order anything."

"Come on," he said, stretching his arms around the huge box, "I'll help you get it inside."

I used an old steak knife I found in the kitchen to saw the top and one whole side of the box open. It took sweat and focus, but after a few minutes, Dylan and I stood in the middle of the living room, staring at what appeared to be a blueberry bush, complete with tag instructions for care and maintenance.

"Why would you give him your address?"

I rolled my eyes. "He's still sending everything to my old address, and then it's forwarded."

Shoving his hands into the wilted leaves, he felt around until he pulled out a paper envelope with a card inside.

"It needs some water." He handed me the card and walked into the kitchen.

On the front of the envelope my name was printed in blue ink. I didn't really want to open the card, so I waited until Dylan returned with a jar full of cold water. Setting it on the coffee table, he said, "Here, hold the box while I pull it out."

The heavy pot slid easily onto the tile and soaked up the jar of water.

Handing the envelope back, I said, "You read it."

Dylan frowned. "I'm not the messenger."

"Then be the interpreter."

With an exasperated sigh, he snatched the envelope from my hand, ripped it open, and read. A few seconds later, his eyes scanned it from top to bottom again. Finally, he ran his tongue over his teeth. "He says he is a ridiculous douchebag liar who thinks he loves you, but couldn't possibly, because he's a ridiculous douchebag liar."

With a straight face, I asked, "He said that?"

Dylan threw the card on the hall table, missed, and didn't bother to pick it up when it fell to the floor. "No. He actually had some stranger at the blueberry bush factory hand-write the lyrics to Champagne Supernova."

"How do you know it's a stranger?"

"Oh, I know," he hoisted the blueberry bush into his arms and walked off down the hall. "It's a girl's handwriting."

Dylan had a way of saying the conversation was over without using words. I knew he wouldn't come back to embellish. I picked up the card and folded it open. Sure enough, "*Someday you will find me…*" printed in curlicue writing with tiny circles to dot the I's, like girls in middle school do. Then, at the bottom, the stranger wrote, "I can't believe you left me, Skye. I love you."

From the kitchen, Dylan yelled, "I resent the fact that douchebag used Oasis to express his phony, self-serving emotions. He soiled one of my favorite songs. Just saying."

I dragged the box through the kitchen and shoved it onto the carport. Then, I dropped the card in the recycling bin. That seemed too easy. Symbolically, I didn't want to recycle the moment. I wanted it to go away. I wanted him to go away. Life was confusing enough without the added dread of selfish professions.

I grabbed the card out of the bin and opened kitchen drawers until I found a box of matches. One strike later, I held the edge of the card to the match, and set it on fire. It sputtered a few times, threatening to fade, but I kept turning the card this way and that, blowing to keep the flame alive. It was an interesting metaphor for my former situation, since no one had fanned flames of love because they were too busy doing nothing.

Maybe we all had it backwards. All that talk about fanning the flames of love. Maybe the flames came at the end, when it burned to the ground. I dropped the flaming card into the stainless steel sink.

Stella walked around the corner, scratching her stomach like a great ape, and asked, "Why is the sink on fire?"

Before I had a chance to explain, Dylan blurted out, "Love note."

"From Trevor?"

"It's not a love note, and it was from my ex. I didn't even hear you pull up. How long have you been here?"

My sister winked. "Silent like ninja. Sexy like bunny."

"It was a total hipster bullshit love note."

I cut my eyes at Dylan and stepped away from the sink. "Well, you'll have to prove it from that pile of ashes."

"I don't need ashes. I can call the company and have them mail a copy of the order. The order number is on the packing slip."

In an attempt to call his bluff, I said, "You wouldn't dare."

"I once drove to Tucson to prove a point."

"Yeah, yeah. I remember."

CHAPTER SEVENTEEN

Taz Minerals and Chakra Clearing was located in a strip mall on the other side of town. Low ceilings and wide tables made it feel flat and spacious in the cool, dim light.

"What are we doing?" I whispered in front of an amethyst cluster.

"Gathering intel," Dylan said, catching sight of an aisle of books around the corner.

A man at the counter looked up from a crystal grid. "Welcome. Let me know if you need any help."

The open shelves were filled with glossy coffee table books full of well photographed, glossy rocks. Rocks of antiquity. Rocks on foreign shores. Rock caves. Rock clusters. And one big stack of bumper stickers that had the store name and said: *Rock on*.

Peeking around the corner to make sure the sales associate was still deeply engrossed in his grid, I leaned into Dylan and whispered, "Are you worried your hair is going to fall out?"

"I'm past that. I was trying to remember the name of something. There's a green stone that is a meteorite, but I can't remember its name."

"Moldavite."

Dylan pinched up his face. "How do you know that?"

I twisted my head all saucy like. "You're not the only one who knows things."

"Huh," he said.

"Stella has a piece in her Zen garden."

"I thought I recognized that rock."

Thumbing through a mineral encyclopedia, I asked, "How long has this store been open?"

"A few years. Why?"

"I think I'll go fill out an application."

"You go, career girl."

Dylan flipped open an illustrated history of rocks. I walked back into the main area.

The sales clerk looked up from pricing a mound of rose quartz. "Can I help you?"

"That's such a loaded question."

"Rough day?"

I glanced at his name tag. Stephen was at least sincere.

"Rough decade."

"Hmmm. Well, can I interest you in a black tourmaline to absorb and redirect negative energy?"

"I'm more interested in a job, actually."

"Oh," his face brightened. "I'm not hiring at the moment, but you could fill out an application." He ducked down, searching under the counter.

"Do you own this place?"

Flipping through folders, he popped his head up. "Yes."

"So, you probably know a lot about rocks."

A deep laugh rose up from behind the counter. "I know a thing or two about rocks, yes."

"What about large, pink rocks?"

Pulling a sheet of paper from a blue folder, he stood up and handed me the application. "Like rose quartz?"

"Kinda. If it glowed."

I picked up a pen from the counter and scanned the application.

"When you say 'glow', do you mean phosphoresce?"

"Maybe." I wrote my name on the top line.

"Are you asking me if rocks glow?"

"Maybe." My eyes drifted down to the questions. Reason for applying? *My bank account has thirty-eight cents in it currently.*

He shrugged. "I suppose anything is possible, but the basic composition of rocks doesn't support glowing, but they are still life. There are some rocks that emit light, and it's possible others exist."

Previous employer?

"There are some stones that glow under black light."

How many years at current address?

"Any that glow pink?"

His eyes drifted to the ceiling. "Hmmm. Fluorite can emit colors under a UV light, but some do glow without a visible light source. There is a less common stone named Eucryptite. The minerals can glow pink under ultraviolet light."

I had to ask, "Are rocks your passion?"

He paused a second, then laughed. "I like to think I am the passion of the rocks."

Dylan popped his head around the corner, "Excuse me, have you ever seen a rock light up?"

Any special skills, hobbies, awards?

"Your friend here just asked me the same question."

"What did you tell her?"

While Stephen repeated rock facts, I finished filling out the application. A depressing walk down memory lane. Dylan set a few books on the counter, along with an impressive geode. I turned in my application. It was like an essay, back to a time I should have never been in.

"At the end of the day," Stephen said, "we're all really just on one big spinning rock."

"True," Dylan said. "What do you like best about rocks?"

"They remember everything. They tell stories, with hieroglyphs and stone tablets, to Mayan calendars and cave paintings. Rocks are the foundation of this world. They are like newspapers of the past."

Dylan lifted his bag full of books. "Get in."

"Get in what?" I asked, turning my head just enough to remove the glare so I could see his face. Communicating with Dylan was a total body experience. I couldn't just hear or feel him. I needed to see him, too. He didn't give everything away with his face, but there were clues. Clues were important.

Shoving aside his bag of books, he said, "In the cart."

A stray shopping cart sat haphazardly in the middle of a parking space. "Why would I want to get in the cart?"

"Because I'm going to push you around."

Not exactly what I had in mind. "I'll pass."

"Come on," he coaxed, heckling me across the parking lot.

Still resisting, I had to know, "Why?"

Dylan stopped, shoulders pinched in a shrug. "Because we used to do it all the time. Because it's fun. Do you really need another reason?"

Dylan's shameless pursuit of fun often left me feeling like all my fun valves didn't fire correctly. I'd become uncomfortable with the girl who went out at 3 AM for tiny hamburgers and fries, or drove out to the middle of the desert and ate under a full moon, with the BBC playing on the phone laying on the roof of the car, like it was waiting for a call from outer space. I'd eaten a lot of food under full moons. Spent a lot of time with Dylan listening to Jim Morrison's spoken word out in the wide-open space of life. But, somewhere, I'd lost something, a piece of me. A rock or pebble or crumb of myself. And, while I couldn't pinpoint it on a map, I instinctually knew it was missing, that I'd taken it out and hidden it, or lost it, or worse, life had stolen it back.

So, I got in the cart.

The rattling was so intense it made my bones feel like they were coming unglued. *Rattle rattle rattle.* Around and around the parking lot we went. Me squealing, Dylan sweating and cheering. Back and forth across the side lot, while a bunch of ravens watched us from a tree.

"Did you find any answers back there?"

"Not a one." Pointing up to the tree, he yelled over the rattling cart noise, "Those birds want to be in the cart with you."

"Birds can fly," I yelled back, my teeth chattering from the bumpy ride.

"So what? Just because you can fly doesn't mean you don't want to participate in fun."

"Then birds should drive."

Wide open road. Wind at your back. Pedal to the floorboard. *Go.* A bliss of silence and sky, that captivating place where stars bend to kiss the Earth and say goodbye, a distance that feels so far away.

Then I saw her.

Actually, I think Dylan saw her first, because he slowed ever so slightly.

Wormy. Getting out of her car wearing faded green scrubs. My hand shot out in front of me before I even thought about what I was going to say. "That way," I yelled.

Dylan hesitated. I felt a slight nudge forward, but the cart didn't move. For most of my exercise in fun I'd been crouched down, holding onto the sides. I stood up and pointed, "That way."

That's when Wormy saw us.

Dylan pushed the cart forward as I did my best to balance, grateful there was no alcohol involved. Wormy glared at me and, even from so far away, I could see she was totally irked. She must have known I was back in town. With the swiftness of a girl on a mission, or at least curious about the competition, Wormy walked toward us.

Behind me, Dylan said something, but I couldn't hear him over the rattle and hum of the cart cutting across empty parking spaces. Wormy had never been a pretty girl, but she knew how to carry herself. She was bigger than me, and Dylan, too, and on some level that should have bothered me. But it didn't, because I was Super Shopping Cart Girl, high on fun and being unemployed. Wormy was tall, so I didn't exactly tower over her, but I had the height advantage standing in the cart.

"Hey, Skye." She shielded her eyes from the sun with her middle finger sticking out. "Still I child, I see."

"Thanks, Wormy. It's good to see you, too."

Shifting her weight from one foot to the other, she pinched her face into a frown. "No one calls me Wormy anymore, bitch."

The sting of the words cut clear through to the blood in my veins. "That's funny, because no one calls me *bitch* anymore."

Dylan ran around to the side of the cart, holding his hands out to stop the fight he was sure was coming. "Okay, ladies. Let's go our separate ways."

Wormy slung an index finger in my direction. "Stay away from Trevor. He doesn't deserve you constantly fucking with his head."

"Fuck you, Wormy."

The one thing Dylan hadn't thought about was that standing next to me, instead of behind me, allowed me to use his shoulder as a jumping-off point. Which I did. Laying my hand flat on his shoulder, I squeezed, and launched myself out of the shopping cart. The cart bolted forward, ramming Wormy in the stomach.

Dylan said, "Uh-oh," out loud, but stayed by my side.

Wormy shoved the cart back at me. "What are you doing? Shopping for other people's husbands?"

"You don't love Trevor."

"That's rich coming from you, Skye. The girl who left him in the middle of the night. You are so narcissistic, you don't know the first thing about the people closest to you, especially Trevor."

"Which only points out that I was there first," because, if it was a competition, then I was going for the win.

"Everything is a game with you."

"You're a liar," I screamed. I was absolutely done hiding the fact that I hated her with every breath.

Her whole body tensed. The cart stood motionless in the space between us.

"You know what you don't get to do?" She asked through narrowed eyes. "You don't get to come back here and screw my husband, and act like everything is cool."

"He won't be your husband for long."

A phone buzzed in her pocket. "You're an asshole, Skye. You always have been. You think because you ran off that you're somehow better than everyone else. You're not. You're the same tragically fucked up girl who got everything she wanted. Well, news flash, princess: the universe doesn't revolve around your angst."

A gigabyte of data actually ran through my mind all at one time, but the only thing I could think to say was, "I am not tragically fucked up."

Wormy glared at me and laughed. A bitter, hot laugh that burned with spite. "Go back to wherever it is you came from."

"I hate you, Wormy," I screamed so loud it made Dylan jump.

Dylan squeezed my arm. "Let's go."

I jammed the cart forward, ramming her thigh, but she slipped around the side and slapped me in the face. I'd never been slapped before. Ever. The burn of her palm striking my face made me pull back my fist and swing. No aim or thought went into throwing a punch. It just felt good. My knuckles landed on her temple, and I heard her scream. Dylan grabbed me around my waist and jerked me backwards so fast, all I could see was the stunned look on Wormy's face as blood dripped down her chin.

How dare she tell me I couldn't have the only man I'd ever loved. How dare she call me tragically fucked up. "Cheater," I screamed, shrill and totally uncool.

Wormy wiped her chin with the back of her hand like a pro wrestler. "What are you talking about?"

"You don't love Trevor."

"So what, Skye? Get over it. You are a clueless little girl who has no idea what love is."

Dylan pulled me backwards, holding tight.

"Says the smug girl from the safety of her bad marriage."

"Get away from me. If you ever touch me again or come near my house, I'll have you arrested."

CHAPTER EIGHTEEN

Dylan drove out to a deserted piece of land guided by a set of coordinates Aaron gave him at the diner. The dry metallic taste of adrenaline hung in my throat. I couldn't breathe or swallow, and my top lip swelled. I wanted something back. Not just Trevor, but all the time I'd lost being away. I'd spent years sitting in groups, talking about my feelings, while everyone else built lives. Maybe it was the wrong life, but it was a life. I was so relieved to see the headlights of Trevor's truck I felt like I was going to burst into tears. I hiked across the uneven terrain to fall into his arms.

He slammed the truck door and stopped. "What the fuck do you think you're doing?"

I shrugged. The current situation didn't exactly call for the level of volatility in his voice. "UFO watching?"

"Don't be cute. Why are you letting Jenny know I'm on to her?"

"Because she was awful."

"Okay, well, let me explain this to you, Skye. In order for me to not get taken in this divorce I need to be able to prove she's cheating on me, which is going to be hard to do since you announced it in a parking lot. Why can't you just shut your mouth and walk the other way?"

"I tried that *once*."

Standoff. Neither one of us moved or blinked. We just stood there, glaring at each other.

Behind me, Dylan crunched through the dry brush and said, "Hey, T-Rex, I've got a roast beef and pickle in the cooler."

"Not now."

"Stop fighting, you two."

Trevor shifted his glare. "You're not the boss of me."

"I'm not even the boss of myself," Dylan snorted. "Lighten up, dude. It wasn't exactly a perfect situation. Trust me, I was there in all its awkward glory. Wormy had it coming."

In my mind, I covered myself head to toe in President of Dylan Wilde's Fan Club buttons.

"Yeah, well, I'm not exactly in a perfect situation now, either. Jenny just left me a sizzling voice mail, then texted me about a hundred times."

Dylan looked into the sky thoughtfully. "Fair enough."

I stood my ground. "I didn't tell her you knew."

"No. You called her a cheater, which is essentially the same thing."

I squeezed the palms of my hands together, "What do you want from me?"

"You know what, Skye? I want you to go back to the summer of 2006 and not leave. How about that? I want you to show me that you actually love me, instead of creating a ton of unnecessary drama every fucking time I need you. How about that? Start there."

"Stop living in the past," I ground my teeth.

"That's where you're living. You're sitting on this strange fence, between the summer you left and the summer you returned, and you don't have a single answer."

"I didn't go away for answers."

"That's obvious."

Ouch.

"You know, I'm not the only one who never pulled it together."

"I'm together," Dylan said, behind me.

"Look, Skye, I appreciate your whole *we're made of Buddha, nothingness and poetry*, and I find it extremely sexy, but I've got a real-world problem, and that is: how to get out of a totally empty marriage, held together with guilt and spite, without losing my ass."

I looked down at the dust, cast in shadow. Trevor's face was a silhouette.

"The 90's are over," Dylan said mournfully.

"I didn't do anything to you," I whispered.

"You kind of did."

"Because I made choices that didn't include you?"

"What the actual fuck, Skye? You can't be serious. You left in the middle of the night with literally no note, no nothing. We walked out into the desert, kissed under the moonlight, pledged our love, found a dead body, and by noon the next day you were gone. You do realize I spent a fair amount of time thinking you were dead? The only girl I'd ever loved disappeared, was gone, possibly dead, and I had a lot of angst about that until my mom died, and all of the sudden I didn't have to speculate. It was real. You do realize it was over a year before I saw Stella, and she told me you'd gone to South Carolina and were okay? And from that single encounter, I spent months knowing you were going to call any second, but you didn't. Like you were seriously going to call, any second. And I don't even know why I expected that from someone who didn't even wait around to find out who the dead body belonged to. In case you care, his name was Lloyd Green, and he was eighty-eight years old, and wandered away from home, and died out here of exhaustion and dehydration. He'd been dead for weeks by the time we found him. So, stop acting like I don't have feelings. I'm not the one challenged by intimacy."

"That's not fair."

"You keep saying that like it means something. No one promised you fairness, and if you can stand there and say what you did to me was fair, then you are more deranged than I imagined."

"What are you faulting me for, exactly? *Leaving?*"

Trevor stood for a moment, backlit by a quarter moon, so angry the tip of his mohawk quivered. "You walked out on me, Skye."

Under that big sky I felt exposed, fraudulent. "We were kids."

"And what is that supposed to mean? Everything that happened under eighteen doesn't count, because you couldn't vote?"

I wholeheartedly did not appreciate the jab.

"Look, the world is full of false hope, Skye. I don't need to get it from the girl I'm standing next to. God, if I want false hope I'll go home and sit in the center of my shitty marriage."

A tiny piece cracked inside me. I couldn't tell where, but I felt it, and that crack flooded me with a ton of emotions I did not want to feel. "You married someone else, Trevor. That wasn't an accident. You can play this off like Skye is the bad guy, but you got down on your knees and asked another girl to marry you, and now, somehow, you want me to forget that ever happened. It's not that easy. You can dump this off on me, but I'm not alone. We all made choices."

Dylan flopped down on his creaky loveseat. "You two are harshing my mellow."

"Thank you, Deepak."

In the shadows, I saw him shrug. "This is the same fight you've been having for a decade."

Trevor laughed. A jaded, sharp laugh.

Dylan popped the top on a Miller High Life. "Look, this is the way I see it: you went east to find meaning. Trevor here got married to find meaning. Neither one of you really hit the mark. Now here you are, all ready to face your choices."

"I didn't go east to find meaning. I went east because I was afraid if I stayed here, I'd be nothing."

"Thanks for the vote of confidence, doll."

"Didn't you ever just want something?" I demanded, angry, squeezing my sweaty palms together, under an emptiness that threatened to unmask me.

"Yeah," Trevor said. "I wanted *you.*"

"That's clever and dramatic, but not the whole truth."

"Fuck you, Skye. It is the whole truth. It just wasn't true for *you.* You spent six years out east with some douchebag because you were afraid you'd be nothing here? That is an absolute load of shit if I've ever heard it."

"*At least I didn't marry him.*"

"It didn't matter what I did, it was never going to be good enough. Married. Unmarried. Waiting. Not waiting. Skye's three-year booty call. You are the reason my grandmother told me to wait to have sex until I was married."

I had so many clever things to say, all of them derailed by his comment. It never occurred to me that guys wanted to wait to have sex. Our entire culture basically sold girls on the idea that's all they wanted. And here he was, in front of me, saying something else. But, like everything with Trevor, I was never sure exactly what that meant.

"That is such bullshit, Trevor. We were young. We had just graduated high school. You're acting like we should have gotten married and started our lives together right then."

"Why not?"

"Because there's a whole world out there."

"How's that whole world working out for you?"

"You know what I mean," I yelled, so totally exasperated I was literally bouncing up and down.

"No. I don't. I'm a simple guy in a very complicated situation. I wanted you and you didn't want me."

"I do want you. You are part of the reason I came back."

"Being part of the reason is so romantic," he snorted.

"Stop twisting my words," I screamed.

"I'm not twisting them. I'm highlighting the insanity of them. Totally different."

"Highlighting the insanity," Dylan whispered from his seat in the dark. "I like that."

"Shut up," I yelled.

Shrugging and exhaling at the same time, Dylan flipped open the cooler and fished around for another beer. "Say what you want, and you know I love you both, but he's got a point."

"So, I should have just not done what I wanted, and stayed here to make everyone feel better?"

Trevor shifted his weight, mohawk tilting to the side, and said, "Go ahead. Tell us what you wanted."

Low blow. Not fair. Foul ball.

Like a twelve-year-old, I yelled, "What do you want?"

Calmly, evenly, he offered, "You first."

"I just wanted to do something different."

"Because doing Trevor was boring. You know, Skye, was the sex with that cheating asshole good? Was the food good? Was the weather better? Were the restaurants posh? Help me out, I'm still struggling to understand why you'd go so far away from me, only to return and claim you felt something for me from the beginning."

"You're acting like I didn't love you."

"You *didn't* love me."

"I did," I screamed.

His lack of emotion made me cry. Big, ugly tears that ran in streams down my cheeks, to be absorbed into the dry desert floor. I didn't have my car, so I couldn't just drive off.

"You are the most selfish person I have ever met, Skye."

"Well, at least I'm consistent."

"Do you actually have feelings under all that clever snark?"

"It's not snark. It's me waking up."

"But you're awake, in the middle of some nightmare you created for yourself, that you can't get out of because you refuse to wake up."

"Thanks, Zen master. That's so helpful."

"I'm not a Zen master. I'm your ex-boyfriend."

"Emphasis on the ex."

"You know, we don't have to do this, Skye. I've got enough problems I've created for myself."

"Did you just call me a 'problem'?"

"You are not the problem. You are some miraculous free zone that I have been in love with my entire adult life. Your inability to get your shit together is *your* problem."

"Because you're such an expert on that."

"At least I made choices. They might have been the wrong choices, but at least I made them. You just hang in this weird limbo where you can't fall down, but no one can get to you, either."

"He has a point," Dylan said from somewhere in the dark.

"Stay out of this," I screamed.

"You want me, but you don't want to believe this is real."

"Because it's not real, Trevor."

"This," he says, gesturing broadly, "this isn't real?"

"Everything between us is some kind of pseudoscience. Like a partially-developed idea one of us dropped, like a three-year-old drops old lollipops."

"Glad to see you brought your emotional age into this."

"This isn't real, Trevor. It doesn't last. It doesn't matter how much I want you."

Trevor grabbed his mohawk and howled. "We can't get to real because you're hovering off somewhere in the *Land of This Might Not Work Out.* All kinds of things don't work, but sometimes they do."

"There's real magic in those moments," Dylan said.

"What would our lives have really been like if I'd stayed?"

"I don't personally know, Skye, because the only thing you've ever been good at is leaving."

Boom. There it was. A truth louder than any truth ever yelled. My skill set, vast and honed.

"And you sucked at that, because you couldn't even make a choice, and spent six years hanging in limbo with some married guy you didn't even like."

"It's good to see we've gotten to the judgment phase of our relationship."

"We don't have a relationship, Skye. You were just a candy-coated girl that sat on my lap and filled me with empty words."

"That's not fair," I screamed. "I loved you."

"People who love each other don't run away."

"No. They marry other people."

"I can see you're upset about Jenny."

"Remember driving around, listening to all those bootleg recordings of Kid Rock at those clubs in Detroit?" Dylan asked from the loveseat.

Trevor and I turned. I was still doing the ugly cry.

Trevor said, "Yes."

"They're in my glove compartment. Go put one in."

"Kid Rock doesn't fix this."

"Don't kid yourself, man. Kid Rock fixes *everything*."

Trevor pawed through the glove compartment and held up CDs in the glimmer of dash light. Twisting the key in the ignition, the dash light illuminated his face. Slipping the CD into the player, he turned to face me. "After Stella told me where you were, I drove to South Carolina and sat outside your house like a *bona fide* stalker. I had a ring and a bouquet of flowers, and I was going to get down on my knees and ask you to marry me."

I was already crying, which saved me the embarrassment of bursting into tears, but not even I was ready for the ocean of emotion that swept over me in that second, an endless second that rippled out across the universe, going forever. A pulse of energy with the endurance to survive.

"And then, some guy pulled up with a guitar, and you kissed him, and my world was over. I drove back, sleeping in my truck at rest areas, changed my oil to focus on something else, and put the ring in a drawer. Later, Jenny found it and assumed it was for her. I don't know who that ring was for. A ghost, maybe."

CHAPTER NINETEEN

I couldn't take my eyes off Trevor, nor could I wipe away the image of him sitting in front of my house a world away.

"Your mailbox was blue, and there was lavender growing in the side yard."

"*Oh, God…*" I whispered.

That tiny piece cracked completely, and in that second, I broke into a thousand pieces, and all the King's horses and all the King's men couldn't put me together again.

"Guys?"

My entire body trembled. *That ring was in the drawer because of me.*

Two glowing balls of light hovered right in front of Dylan, so close he could touch them with his hand. And he did. My eyes popped open so wide I felt the corners stretch. The bed of his truck was fully lit, and his blue eyes sparkled.

Trevor's whole body relaxed, his shoulders looking like they were going to melt to the ground. There, in the middle of the glow, sat Dylan, illuminated with silver sparkle.

"Oh, my God," I whispered, because saying unintelligent things on the precipice of profound moments was my trademark.

The light flitted around Dylan's fingers, and he stood up, a wild sage in a labyrinth, taming spirits with touch. A zap of electricity shot out from one light and made contact with Dylan's thumb.

Someone yelled. "Skye!"

It sounded like Dylan, but everything was dark. I blinked my eyes. The world around me came into focus.

"What the actual fuck?" Trevor yelled. "Where are we?"

Dylan glowed in front of me. Lights swung wildly around my head, so fast I couldn't make out their shapes. Dim light filtered through enormous trees that rose from the earth like giants.

"The Redwood Forest," I yelled. "My parents took us there when I was in high school."

So alive, so old. An ancient heartbeat hummed through the wild spinning of the planet. The forest surrounding us was like a hologram. Beyond the trees, craggy mountains rose from the desert earth. In the middle of a memory projected in the desert we stood stunned, in silence, watching the lights. A feeling of magnificent calm filled my mind. Suddenly, I forgot about the lights, and letting go, and fighting with Trevor. I forgot every worried detail.

Stella gave a surprised scream. I turned, shocked to see a glowing image of my sister. Four years older and already in college, she danced around me like a fairy in a circle, the fringe of her leather bag flopping up and down. I stared at her, amazed, seeing right through her body.

"We should hold an ancient ceremony," she sang out loud.

Noise like a helicopter engulfed us, and the lights spun faster.

"Oh, my God," Dylan yelled. "this is incredible."

"Can you see my sister?" I yelled back.

Trevor held his arms out, turning in a circle like some sacrificial rock god. "This cannot be happening."

The noise died down, the quiet *whomp whomp* of light spinning.

"Yes," Dylan's laughter rang out, "this is totally happening. I can see Stella."

"You realize we're all probably lying unconscious in the desert right now," Trevor yelled.

Dylan ran in a circle beneath the rings of light. "Isn't this glorious?"

The look of utter bliss on his face gave me reason to pause.

"We're going to be eaten by coyotes," Trevor yelled.

Maybe this wasn't the moment I'd waited my entire life for, and maybe it wasn't the exact moment Dylan was waiting for, but it was close. I knew my future was in this place. For the very first time in my life, I could feel the gentle unfolding of destiny. It was trippy and bizarre. Standing inside the projection of the Redwood Forest, Dylan held his arms out wide and danced with the unknown.

"Let's make a forest message," Stella said.

"Forest message?" Dylan asked.

Stella looked at me. It was an exact replay of the real event. A movie, playing around me. "Let's take the twigs and rocks and leaves and write a message for the trees to watch over. Something we want. This great tribe of trees will hold the magic," transparent Stella said.

I looked over at Trevor, who was watching Stella. Then, to my utter surprise, I saw the faintest image of myself kneeling in the forest.

Stella was unbearably practical, but sometimes she stepped over the edge and surprised me. My sister. The redneck mystic. The image of me flickered. I stood in the desert and watched myself gather a twig here, a skinny leaf there. I knew exactly what that image was thinking. I'd met Trevor at a midnight showing of Harold and Maude at the art-house theater months before. I hadn't thought about anything else since.

Dylan reveled in the champagne supernova above his head, but Trevor drifted over to stand behind the image of me. I couldn't blame him. A secret clue is a valuable thing to possess. I knew what I was writing in the Redwood Forest.

Under slender rays of sunlight, I'd taken a stick and carved in the dirt:

Trevor.

I took leaves and seeds and buds and created a frame around my declaration.

Trevor's face changed and softened, like he'd known all along. Like now, he could be sure. Like I'd redeemed myself with dirt and a stick and honesty. I wanted to stay right there and kiss him. Get swept into the bliss of whatever this mind-bending thing was, but I turned and followed the image of my sister off to the side. I'd always known what I asked the forest spirits to grant. But I'd left that day, high on miracles and tribes of trees, and never once thought to look at what my sister had written. I swung wide to see what she'd asked for. There, in the middle of some incredible mass hallucination, I saw the weirdest part of all.

A small altar was built around a block of words where she wrote:

Give my wish to Skye.

A message written long ago. A message on what I now saw was one of the most important days of my life.

Stella. Four years older. One solid universe wiser. I leaned my head way back, letting my eyes travel up the length of trees, way, way, way up to the sky, where the enormity of it all made me so dizzy I fell backwards to the ground.

An ancient heartbeat hummed through the center of a wild, spinning planet. Everything rose from the earth.

Dust.

Trevor.

Trees.

Keepers of secrets.

Spinning lights that went *whomp whomp whomp* deep in my chest.

"What is this?" Dylan exclaimed.

I turned my head, dust and grit sticking to my cheeks. Trevor was still hunched over my forest message. Dozens of lights descended from the sky. Euphoric breath filled my lungs.

I laughed out loud, and Dylan looked over and yelled, "Are you okay?"

Sophomore year. The rich smell of bark and dirt. Leaves warmed in sunlight. Three weeks from now, I'd go on a hot date with the guy nine feet away.

I felt Trevor's hand on my back and thought I was dreaming. The wind roared. Dust kicked up and Dylan swung, deliriously, in circles, until all at once, the lights shot straight up into the sky. Heartbeat and breath were the only sounds.

Dylan waved dust from his face. "You saw that, right?"

Trevor whooped so loud it gave me chills.

"Please, God, tell me someone got that on video."

"I left my phone back at the truck," I said.

Trevor held his in the air. "Mine's fried."

Dylan groaned loudly, turning in a circle. "Whoa, where are we?"

I looked left, then right. The trucks were gone.

"You're the one who read all those Jack London books. You should have supreme navigation skills," I said.

Dylan smacked his lips and set off in the direction of the moon. "So I did."

Everyone has moments they'll remember forever.

Simple truths.

The majesty of beauty.

The equation of us.

That was one of mine.

Dylan fell face first into a pile of scrub brush, and I stumbled forward to give him a hand. Disorientation was real. The memory. The darkness. The fact that in all that chaos, we'd obviously walked so far from the trucks we were lost.

Dusting himself off, Dylan threw his head back and let out a tremendous howl. It was his superpower. Not letting shit get to him.

Turning to me, he said, "Try it."

"Try what?"

"Howl."

"It's my favorite poem."

"Nice dodge."

I could feel Trevor standing off to the side, too far to touch. I didn't want to touch him. I wanted to *touch* him. I was just about to when, up ahead, I saw a road.

"Civilization on the horizon."

Trevor walked around me.

Dylan ran to the shoulder.

Blazing through unfamiliar terrain fried my circuits. Asphalt is a wondrous invention. Even more so when you're lost in the desert in the middle of the night with your best friend and ex-boyfriend. Because nothing screams friendship like mass hallucination.

"Where are we?" I asked, turning in a circle on the yellow line.

Trevor inhaled, but didn't say anything.

"I don't know," Dylan said. "I've been out here a lot, but I don't know how far we wandered after we saw the lights."

"I've been wandering my whole life."

"That is an extremely accurate summation of your personal life, but it's not going to help us find our way back."

"Which one is the North Star?" Trevor asked.

We all tilted our heads back to stare up into the sky. An army of stars overhead. Sentries of the night. Trudging through the dark gave me a lot of time to think about me and Stella in the Redwood Forest. A sliver of moonlight hung high in the sky. Not enough to light our way. Just something to be admired.

"I think that's it," Dylan pointed and turned, "which means town would be that way."

Trevor set off in that direction, his combat boots clomping on the road. I pulled up the rear.

The romantic notion of taking to a highway at night is underrated. The long walk, the distance combined with the disorientation makes it a soulful moment.

"Has anyone ever seen this road before?" Dylan asked.

"I've seen it a few times," Trevor said. "I think we're headed in the right direction."

First time for everything. I'm headed in the right direction.
"I have to ask: did we all just experience my memory?"

Up ahead, Dylan nodded. "Looks that way."

"What do you think that means?"

"That the meaning of life is somewhere in all these details."

"That we're linked?"

"Well, that's obvious."

The wide-open space felt like the entire world was constructed of mere possibility. Terrifying but liberating. Not a single headlight flashed on the road. The world was totally empty except for us. Footsteps and breath and possibility. I could feel Dylan thinking. It was like air crackling around his head, little electrical charges zapped out into the night every time he contemplated a new thought. I wanted Trevor to speak, but I was tired of words designed to fit in the tight spaces between silence and darkness. I'd had a lifetime of idle chit-chat. A deep pit in my stomach opened up and swallowed the thought that Trevor and I were over. Like, not just running away, but calling it quits. God, I had so totally screwed everything up. I saw that clearly.

The edges of Trevor glowed in the scant light up ahead.

"I have seen some really freaky things," Dylan said, "but that Redwood Forest wins the prize."

"No one has any clue what is actually happening on the surface of this planet," Trevor said.

"Amen, brother."

It had been a long time since I'd hiked that far. There was freedom in deep breaths. Maybe not the ones standing on a mat in a stifling hot room, but out there, deep breaths were a passionate declaration. Dylan whooped. Up ahead, on a service road, illuminated by one streetlight, was an old gas station. Everyone picked up their pace, especially Trevor, who obviously didn't want to fall into step beside me. I thought him seeing my declaration would somehow transmute his anger, but it hadn't happened.

I was about to run past both of them when, up ahead, under the glow of the gas station sign, I saw Charlie. Quiet and confident she sat, poised with her furry butt hitched to the side. The night was quiet and warm, and the sound of our footsteps lulled me into a trance.

Trevor glanced back at Dylan. I knew he'd seen Charlie, even though I couldn't see his face. I was delirious from lack of sleep and memories and the choking vines of a past I struggled to escape. I was delirious from not being able to explain anything. Maybe I was delirious because I constantly felt like I had to explain everything. Dylan reached back for my hand.

Standing in the middle of the street, Charlie sat illuminated by light overhead. It felt like slow motion as we stopped and stared. Charlie had never looked so real. As we inched closer, I could see the otherworldly edges of her body. After a bit of focus, I realized I could see right through her. An ethereal dog. Her see-through nature didn't bother her a bit. She sat quietly and wagged her tail.

Trevor and I slowed to a stop, but Dylan kept walking. A few inches away, he knelt down and looked her in the eye.

"Charlie?" he whispered.

In the warm glow of light, she wagged her tail again.

"Hey, girl, I've missed you. No one eats Grape Nuts with me anymore. Well, Skye would eat them if I asked, but it's not the same."

Charlie curled her lip up in a funny dog smile.

"I knew it was you. I knew it," Dylan whispered, in a tone that suggested even he couldn't believe it was happening. "I know you're trying to tell me something. Is it about that rock I found in the desert?"

Only Dylan could have a serious conversation about a meteorite with a phantom dog.

It annoyed me.

I was lost in the desert, with Trevor refusing to make eye contact, and instead of me having an epiphanous moment, Dylan was plunged into the center of a strange riddle. *His riddle.* His dog, his lights in the sky, his quest to solve the mystery of life. I was just along for the ride. A hitchhiker in the live-action version of his life. An extra on the set of Dylan's life story.

Trevor must have felt my angst because he reached for my hand and squeezed. Not a I-forgive-you squeeze, but an I-need-a-buddy-in-this-moment-of-insanity squeeze. Inhaling and closing my eyes at the same time made me feel like I was floating. I could float if I could just let go.

Charlie stood up and walked down the center of the street, silhouetted by the moon. An old outbuilding stood on the side of the gas station. Dylan followed Charlie across the dusty patch of land that led to the back. I wanted to keep floating, but Trevor pulled me forward. Dylan rounded a corner up ahead, concealed by the outbuilding. Walking and breathing took every bit of energy I had left. Trevor broke into a run trying to catch up to Dylan. I picked up speed, but felt like I was filled with cement.

I let go of Trevor's hand, only because I was too tired to keep up.

Charlie walked to the side of the outbuilding and sat down in the moonlight. It took me a second to catch up, but when I did, I saw that beside her, an old, skinny dog sat upright. Charlie looked at Dylan, then the dog, and started to fade.

Right in front of us.

I'd grown to like phantom Charlie and didn't want to see her fade. One minute, she looked startlingly real. The next minute, she disappeared like the past. Then, with ease and intent, Charlie walked straight into the other dog and merged. I couldn't take my eyes off her small black body until there was nothing but the patchy fur of a homeless dog.

The disappearance left Dylan face-to-face with what I believed was a real dog. Sad and lonely, but with enough spirit to lift a paw and shake.

Dylan looked back over his shoulder at us. "I'm going to name him Buck."

The road to enlightenment, as far as I could see, was populated with one girl so exhausted she could cry, two guys who'd been chasing phantom dogs and lights in the sky, and one old dog recently christened Buck. I don't know who was more tired, me or the dog. I felt like I hadn't really slept since South Carolina. Like I existed on catnaps and candy bars.

Miles rolled away with our weary steps, until some guy on his way to town let us ride in the back of his truck. Everything was exactly as we left it. Truck doors open, cooler on the ground.

Dylan loaded Buck into the front seat and checked the rock. "Come on, you two. We'll crash at my place."

The glorious relief of lying flat on Dylan's sofa made my entire body sigh. An amazing exhalation of stress and over stimulation escaped as I closed my eyes and fell asleep in the middle of the desert with a dog named Buck.

CHAPTER TWENTY

I opened my eyes to find Dylan standing over me, holding two hot dogs in each hand. A hula girl collection lined a shelf over the window. The enticing scent of mystery meat shoved in a warm bun made my stomach growl. Laying half on, half off the sofa, sprawled out like I'd dropped from the sky. Trevor had fallen asleep on the floor, but now a blanket folded on a wicker chair was the only proof he'd ever been there.

Every year me and Stella went to the fair with our parents. I was hot dog funnel cake girl. Stella was French fry Sno-Cone girl.

Dylan knelt down and gave Buck one of the hot dogs. It was gone in three chomps. Buck wandered over to an ice bucket full of water and rounded off his dining experience with a cold beverage.

Rubbing my eyes, I said, "No onions, sauerkraut, relish, mustard, cheese?"

Raising an eyebrow, he said, "Sure you're up for a super-duper Dylan special?"

"I spent the entire night in the Twilight Zone. I'm famished."

"Challenge accepted. Strange nights with weird lights call for chili. Let me see if I can find a can."

I wandered out front to stretch, and realized Trevor was still there.

"Hey," I said casually, trying to be cool and not fall to pieces next to the nice lawn furniture.

He cocked his half-flattened mohawk and dropped his sunglasses to the tip of his nose.

"Don't look at me like that."

"Like what?"

"With your stare of disapproval."

"I don't have a stare of disapproval, Skye."

"Yeah, you do."

Pushing his glasses back up with his thumb, he resumed his position on the chaise. Everything felt so done, so over. Like nothing would ever move forward because I couldn't get past one moment, and I couldn't quite pinpoint that moment. But there *was* a moment. I'd been circling it my entire adult life, like the perfect parking space in the full shopping mall of life. Round and round I went.

"I should have gone to college," I said.

"If you say so."

"Don't you think I'm just going in circles?"

"I think you're standing still."

I wanted to pummel Trevor. Like, pick up the fancy teak end table and slap him in the face. Because you don't get to be right constantly without consequences.

Ugh.

Right?

I didn't know what else to do, so I took off running. The hike back to civilization had made me achy and exhausted, but also reminded me I was alive. I dodged rocks and scrubby little brush and ran. I heard the chaise scrape against the ground, and Trevor's boots pounding.

He hated running. I felt certain he'd give up. Not me. I kept running and running, dodging everything in my path until I was so thirsty, I felt like I couldn't breathe. I circled back around to Dylan's front yard, feeling crazy and alone. Bent over, trying to catch my breath, I knew I was acting psycho, but I couldn't stop.

Trevor must have been well-hydrated, because when he caught up with me, he just looked annoyed. "Is this a performance piece you put together to actually show me what you're thinking every time you're near me?"

"I'm jogging. Normal people jog."

"You're running away from me."

"God, you think everything is about you."

"Most of life isn't about me, Skye, but the parts that are get all my attention."

Sweaty and out of breath, I backed away, noticing I smelled like a truck driver after a cross-country run.

"I know you're never going to get over Wormy, and maybe I really screwed that up, but that came after."

"After what?"

"After you left. It's just me and you out here. I want you to tell me why you really left. No bullshit. No lies. No embellishing the truth to make me feel better. Tell me. I'm not the kinda guy who feels the world owes him something, but you owe me that."

"I thought we wouldn't be together. I thought you'd marry someone else."

"I did."

"Did what?"

"I married someone else."

The past, present, future collided in an atom-smashing moment.

Maybe…

I just…

"Maybe you're like André and see things. Maybe you saw exactly what was going to happen, because you knew exactly what you were going to do."

"No," I said, but it was a reaction to an uncomfortable moment, not the truth.

"Maybe it was always going to happen like this. Maybe I didn't want you to see me weak and shell-shocked because my mom was murdered. Maybe I vibed you away so you wouldn't see the dirty, terrible parts. Maybe you and I are so connected we repelled each other in an effort to live through the awful, without dragging the other one through our shit."

None of this had ever occurred to me. I'd always just assumed his love for me would fade and Trevor would find someone else.

What if I was that someone else?

What if I'd never been falling apart?

What if I'd just been shedding the thousand skins that never fit me?

"What does our future look like?"

He shrugged, the front of his tee wet with sweat. "I don't know. I've never been able to get you to love me in the present."

"I do love you," I blurted. "I do."

"I don't think I've ever met someone so wonderfully stuck in their own head."

What if everything had been falling into place, piece after piece, this entire time?

Maybe this was real. Maybe it was the beginning, not the end.

I hung all my hope on one guy. I wasn't the first person to do it. Guys do it, too. Hang all their hopes on a girl. And it's not just opposite sex. It's same sex. We're all out there, clinging to the notion that relationships must work out, or they don't matter. They do matter. Even the busted, broken, aimless, stupid ones matter.

Even the one in South Carolina. I believed I'd met the man of my dreams but he turned out to be a total fraud. A liar of the highest order. I fell for it, my heart on fire, the cheering section in my brain working overtime. I crisscrossed highways of unfamiliar states, and I believed I'd found love. The truth was I'd found the greatest of lies. An online charlatan. Mr. Right was all clever text and tell-me-your-secrets in an email. The harsher truth was that I could not turn around and drive away. I could not face Dylan, or my sister, or my parents, and especially not Trevor. They say the path you take to escape your destiny leads you straight to it. I would have argued that before, but standing out in a blazing desert trying to make sense of a summer brought the world at large into focus.

I'd been a selfish, silly girl. I'd made mistakes. I'd let go of the right things and held onto the wrong things far too long. But there I was, back at the beginning, fresh-faced, tear-stained, confused, and ready to do it all again.

Differently.

We don't get many second chances in life, so I took that one. At the very root of our lives is a question. That one question is like a spring where other questions form. That form gives rise to our quest. The quest is full of obsessions and mysteries, driven by desire to new avenues that branch off in all directions. The direction we take dictates the story we tell ourselves. And others. But especially ourselves. In the center of these stories lies the nature of reality. Inside that is the meaning of our lives.

But enough of that bullshit. I was ready to let go.

"I met him on the internet," I blurted out.

Trevor cocked his head. "Who?"

"Ethan."

I wanted to cry. The pressure building in my chest made me feel like I was going to explode.

"Who's Ethan?"

"The guy. The guy from South Carolina."

What little smile lingered on Trevor's face disappeared. The sun was incredibly hot, hotter than usual.

"What are you saying, Skye?"

I sucked in a huge breath. The moment I'd been careening away from for six years came to a dead halt right in front of me. I could not get around it anymore. I had to tell Trevor the truth. Maybe I didn't owe him anything else, but I owed him the truth.

"I met him on the internet. He's the reason I went to South Carolina. To be with him."

I think I would have handled it better if I could have seen his eyes, seen him blink, but his aviators were so dark I couldn't see his eyes.

Just a cold stare.

He opened his mouth to speak, but a smirk pulled his attention away and he stopped. Then, I got my wish.

Dropping his sunglasses to the tip of his nose, he looked me in the eye and said, "You were two-timing me? The whole time?"

"We were seventeen, Trevor."

"No," he pointed, "you were seventeen. I was old enough to know better."

"You're really going to make a big deal about this?"

"Why are you even telling me this now?"

"Because it's the truth."

"So, lemme see if I understand this: while I was off pining for you and thinking, *believing,* you were the girl of my dreams, you were flirting with some married guy in South Carolina?"

"I didn't know he was married until after I got there."

"You defend that point like it in some way makes sense of your insanity."

"It's not going to make sense. It's just something I did, and I wish I hadn't, and here I am, and I felt like I owed you an explanation."

Trevor pushed the aviator glasses back into place. "Come on, Skye. If we've learned anything from all this, it's that you don't owe me anything."

Straight for the heart.

Boom.

I should have known.

Trevor was funny and kind and romantic and sexy, but I'd never seen him forgive anyone. Not even Dylan. And he wasn't going to forgive me. But I had to tell him. I was so fucking mad about Wormy because I'd dropped Trevor and Wormy caught him. She wasn't the better girl. She was in the right place at the right time, and she'd gotten the ring. It was exactly how I felt about Ethan's wife. A ridiculous cosmic cycle I couldn't get out of.

Trevor walked over and jerked the driver's door on his truck open. Without saying a word, he climbed inside and drove away without ever looking back.

That was Trevor's superpower.

Never looking back.

My kryptonite.

Looking back held me in a weird limbo. Static. The old gray fuzz on TV screens when the cable went out.

There I was.

Standing in the desert of my youth.

Still not grown up.

But trying.

Because, for the first time in my life, I really, really wanted something I was pretty sure I'd never get.

And I cried.

Like big, dumb, ugly-face alligator tears.

I cried for the past I couldn't correct, and a future that was little more than history.

CHAPTER TWENTY-ONE

My ex-boyfriend sat in the shade of the porch, staring down at his phone.

Dylan pulled into my sister's driveway and raised an eyebrow. "Looks like somebody learned how to use a search engine."

"Oh, God," I exhaled, but really, I wanted to throw my face into the dash over and over, until all the stupid in my life evaporated.

"You need backup?"

"No," I groaned. I was just grateful Trevor wasn't in the truck to talk shit about me when they pulled away.

Dylan pulled his sunglasses down, peering over the top rim like a disapproving church lady. "Looks like a douchebag, but I bet he has a really nice car."

"You're an asshole."

"Lexus or Audi?"

I rolled my eyes, reaching for the door handle. "Audi."

"Ha," he whooped. "I should have bet money on that one."

Ethan smiled when he saw me, but it quickly faded. People talk about how hard it is to fake an orgasm, but faking sincerity is absolutely brutal. Worse, no one wants to talk about faking sincerity because it's done all day, every day, by everyone. Women in unfulfilling relationships make good talk-show fodder. Speaking of unfulfilling relationships, mine was standing right in front of me.

Instead of feigning nice or, at the very least, concerned, I blurted out, "What are you doing here?"

Totally legit question. I don't care what anyone says.

His smile drooped and he sighed. "I was worried about you, Skye. You left in the middle of the night."

"I also left a note."

"A paragraph doesn't really sum up years, does it?"

"Ummm, yeah, it kinda does." The *burn, pop, sizzle, snap* of sarcasm gobbled up the air between us. My throat went dry. *The truth.* A real intimacy killer.

"You can be so cruel, Skye."

"Says the man who's been leaving his wife for five years."

Dylan honked loudly and backed out of the driveway. A few beetles skittered across the asphalt, but I noticed most of them were gone. Even the bugs weren't tragic enough to stick around for my reckoning.

"I can see you haven't given up your hostile self."

"My inner child has a sword."

"Just because you're done doesn't mean I am."

"Don't be psycho."

"So, you just get to leave? Is that it? And you don't care what I have to say?"

Talking to him was the single most exhausting thing I'd ever done. "I care what you have to say, but I don't know why you're saying it. Look, if we were going to get married, we'd be married."

"Is that what you want? Because I'll get down on my knee right here."

"No. Stop."

Lowering himself to one knee, he balanced and said, "Skye—,"

"Stop."

"Stop what?"

"This. You're making this all about me, like I'm some damaged blow-up doll that can't feel. Ethan, *you have a wife.* Not only that, you're flirting with girls in messages CONSTANTLY. I saw them. You're doing that because you can't admit that all your relationships, up until now, are wrong for you." Moment of extreme clarity. They didn't come often, but when one arrived, it was a game-changer. "You're acting like this is all me. Like Skye is broken. Skye can't handle reality."

"So, now I can't email any girl ever?"

"You're such a fucking liar. Stop dodging reality so you can get out of this."

"Really, Skye? You're worried that I'm dodging reality? What have you been doing for the last few years in that expensive bungalow I pay for?"

"Eating granola and writing bad poetry." Because, when going for the win, the absurd but true statements can't be challenged.

Inhaling slowly, he said, "You are a piece of work."

"You're a dick, Ethan, and a liar. I might be confused and airy-fairy, but I never lied to you."

"Did it ever occur to you that maybe the reason I never busted up my marriage is because you didn't have the guts to tell me you love me?"

"Because I don't. Why do you think I left?"

"Because leaving is what you're good at."

Poison arrow to the heart. The brutal, raw truth fileted me. "Yeah, well, Ethan, if that's true, then all I have to do is find something worth holding onto. You, on the other hand, will be a lying cheater forever."

"Maybe I just never found the right girl."

"Is that supposed to sting?"

To my complete surprise, he laughed in my face. "Oh, Skye. I should have thrown you back. You are still a child."

"Well, now you don't have to babysit me."

What was I thinking? Cinnamon vodka shots. A charming older man. The moon cascading over the surface of the ocean at the end of the pier. Dizzy and drunk on an unfamiliar world that held promise. Shooting stars in the wide-open night.

I'd closed my eyes.

And wished.

I wished to fall in love.

I should have known it wasn't going to be the guy right in front of me. Wishes are complicated. Wishes are full of responsibility and wonder. And they come true. When you least expect it. And they burn a trail of destruction straight to the fire in your heart. At least, mine did.

"Will you at least take me back to the airport," he squinted into the sun.

If I said yes, it meant I had to go inside and get my keys. I was torn. I wanted to go on being completely indignant over the fact that he and I just never clicked, never hit that groove, never slipped deep into each other. But, if it wasn't my fault, then it wasn't his, either, and I could be indignant all day. It didn't change the fact that two people not meant for each other would never be together at the end of the day, regardless of how much shade I threw in his direction. We just stood there, staring at each other, as the past rolled away like tumbleweed.

"I knew you wouldn't come back," he said quietly. "I just came to make sure you're okay. Maybe you didn't love me, but I loved you."

"It doesn't work that way."

"You're not an expert on love, Skye."

Boom. Pop. Sizzle.

Because he was right about one thing, I dodged the bullet and said simply, "I'll drive you to the airport."

The cool, dim hallway was welcome after arguing in the sun. I'd spent a lifetime arguing under a blaze of furious light. I was supposed to be smarter because of it, more self-assured. I was supposed to learn something. What doesn't kill you makes you *blah blah blah.*

I left Ethan standing in the living room and went to find my keys. The second I saw my bed, I wanted to pull my pillow over my head and sleep for a month. I was grimy and hadn't showered. I needed cool water and soft sheets. I needed to figure out my life.

My keys were on the nightstand.

A door slammed and, for the briefest moment, I thought maybe I'd been freed from driving to the airport.

"Hey, baby sister," Stella sang out.

Wanting to intercept her before she rounded the corner into the living room, I grabbed my keys swiftly and stepped into the hall, where I heard Stella say, "Oh, hi. Who are you?"

In true correctional officer form, Stella had drawn her weapon. It was one thing to ask someone who they are, another thing altogether to be prepared for the answer.

Ethan was positively horrified, and actually reached for me as I rounded the corner.

"Put your firepower away. It's just my ex."

"Your ex?" she said, slipping her 9mm into her holster, under her favorite faux-snakeskin jacket.

"The guy from South Carolina."

"Oh, right." Her whole face beamed with rumor and innuendo. "What's he doing in the living room?"

"*The guy from South Carolina*," Ethan repeated, dismissively. In a startling turn of events, he dropped his wounded routine and said simply, "I came to say goodbye."

The truth was as jarring to Stella as it was to me. My sister stood there, blinking at him in a way normally reserved for drunks and idiots.

"Okay," she said slowly. "You could have sent a card."

Pointing to the corner of the living room, he said, "I sent a blueberry bush. Though not for goodbye, really. Skye and I used to pick blueberries together."

"Once. We picked blueberries once," I corrected.

"It was beautiful," he said, in a way that would've made Proust proud.

Stella inhaled deeply and said, "My sister is the most beautiful person I've ever met, and I picked blueberries with her first."

Ethan stared at me with this over-romanticized expression. "She is," he agreed.

The whole thing was so weird I wanted to scream. My sister and I had never been diabolically opposed to each other, but she'd never been my knight in shining armor, either. I couldn't explain Ethan. I couldn't explain the last twenty-four hours of my life. *Who was I kidding? I couldn't explain the last decade of my life.*

Stella grabbed my shoulder briskly and said, "I need to talk to my sister a minute."

Down the hall we went. Stella and I crammed into the bathroom and closed the door. The walls were bright blue. Her dirty socks were everywhere.

"Where have you been?"

"It really is a long story."

"You just sorta vanish, Skye, and make people worry. You have to stop doing that."

"I learned it from you."

She huffed and gave me the stink eye. "I've got a few things in the works. I promise to stop being so cryptic. It's just complicated."

Being reprimanded by my sister always made me feel eight years old, so I stood there, blinking.

"Where's Trevor?"

"He went to work."

"Is everything okay with him?"

"Last I checked he was never going to speak to me again."

Stella exhaled loudly. "And now there's a dude in our living room."

The old *dude-in-our-living-room* problem. The fact that I was really good at disappearing settled over me. Like something I could take pride in. I'd never really been good at anything, except matching my clothes and wearing eyeliner. I was good at walking out on people. *Like, really good*. Like I needed a blue ribbon to hang from my neck that said: I will walk out on you better than anyone else.

Stella raised an eyebrow and reached up to hold onto the shower rod. "Do you want me to drive him to the airport?"

It was part of what I loved about my sister. Her ability to go straight to blunt. Zero to blunt in, like, three seconds. Never small talk girl. The one to make you feel better about your dumb choices.

I inhaled fast and exhaled slow, like fake medics teach people to do on TV shows. Gain perspective. Regain balance. Keep moving forward.

"Okay," I said, inhaling again. "Just give me a minute alone."

Stella laughed. "Is he really worth a minute?"

The very tone of her voice could have splintered bone.

"No. And he wasn't worth six years, which is why I'm crammed in a bathroom with you, whispering. But I'd like to bring some sort of conclusion to that temporary lapse in sanity, so we can all move on."

Looking me up and down, she pulled her bottom lip tight, kicked a few of her dirty socks behind the toilet, and said, "Fair enough. I'll be waiting outside."

And, just like that, she squeezed past me and went into the hall, where she walked out to the driveway to wait in her car. People spend a decent amount of time looking in the mirror, preparing for all the awards they'll accept, or smiles they'll flash at strangers who will fall in love with them, but almost no one stops to glance in the mirror to see what their face looks like when they say goodbye.

Ethan smiled when I stepped back into the living room. A chirpy, *laissez-faire* smile he'd perfected, but it was too tight around the edges to be convincing. I wasn't perfect. Maybe I'd struggled with that for a long time. It seemed like I'd built up this huge list of things I wanted for my life and hit bottom every time I fell short. But, maybe the real art to living had nothing to do with acceptance or accomplishment or goals. Maybe real living is elevated to a piece of divinity when forced into place by natural abandon.

Abandon all hope.

Jump off that ship of fools.

You were wrong for me. Totally wrong in every way.

That's okay.

Staying won't make it right.

"Go back to your wife, Ethan."

His whole face went slack, forcing the tight smile to vanish. "You don't mean that," he said, slowly.

"I absolutely do. And if you don't want to make your marriage work then, at the very least, turn her loose so she can find happiness."

"What a Deepak moment."

"You make fun of me, but I'm right."

"So, you're turning me loose so I can find happiness?" He asked, with an edge so bitter it burned.

I looked at him flatly and said, "I'm turning you loose because I don't love you."

His fists tightened like a man who wanted to break everything in sight, especially me. But I didn't care anymore. Maybe I couldn't take care of myself, but my sister could give anyone a proper ass-whooping. This would be the second ex she ass-whooped in the front yard, if I was counting.

"Stella will give you a ride to the airport."

In that classic way every psycho chooses when dumped, he asked smugly, "Are you sure you trust me alone in a car with your sister?"

It was my turn to smile. A genuine *fuck you* smile. "She works for the Department of Corrections. You'll be fine. Just keep your hands to yourself."

It's hard to imagine what kind of asshole a person will be when you break up with them, but every fight we'd ever had flashed through my mind in an instant, and I realized that Ethan had always been a liar, always hiding something from someone in a pathological display of brokenness. His wife. Me. The endless trail of girls instant messaged, emailed, chatted. Like flirting to find someone better was his drug. An endless litany of clever replies to avoid the fact that, in the real world, sometimes you have parsley stuck in your teeth, and your stomach cramps, and you're totally fucking over traffic. Ethan was broken. In that staggering moment, I had to adult harder than I'd ever adulted before and be the one to inflict the final blow.

What we want to say in our head comes out so perfectly when we're lying in bed, staring at shadows on the ceiling. A perfect cascade of snarky replies and enlightened observations, that fizzle like an old candle wick under the stress of real life. It wasn't like I didn't know what to say. I'd spent days driving across the country, thinking about nothing but what I was going to say to Ethan. Some of that changed when I realized I was in love with Trevor, had always been in love with Trevor.

No one tells you that if it's broken you can't fix it, because no one wants to be thrown away. I'd spent my whole life in some imaginary world where I could pretend to like people I could never love, because it was a lot safer than running full-throttle into Trevor's arms. Trevor was a train wreck who couldn't match his socks, and frequently went commando, because laundry was more optional than imperative. For some reason, I'd woken up one day, lost my mind, and thought I'd be more successful if I didn't love him.

And I drove away.

For six long years.

And the ordeal in the living room was all I had to show for it. Damn. That was hard.

"You have to go," I said. "It's nothing personal."

"You are unbelievable, Skye. Was everything a big lie to you? Were you just full of pretty words?"

I looked at him flatly, and said, "Lies are never pretty, Ethan. Don't be a dick."

Dylan rounded the corner and found me in the carport, hunched over my trunk, crying.

"Hey, cupcake. Want a shoulder?"

I turned and screamed at the same time, startled and sad. "What are you doing here?"

Blowing air into his cheeks like a little kid, he stuffed his hands into his pockets. "I couldn't really leave you here. That's not really what friends are for. Real friends hide in the side yard and eavesdrop." He raised his eyebrows and shrugged.

My shoulders slumped forward. I felt guilty and overwhelmed that my ex sullied my desert dwelling.

Dylan looked at me, then down into the trunk. "How are the mice?"

"They think ex-boyfriends are dumb."

"So do I," he smiled. "That's why I don't have any."

"You're lucky." I wiped my eyes. I was tired of feeling sorry for myself. It was pointless. An exhausting few days full of questions got me nowhere.

"Stop being so hard on yourself. You're not the sum total of every shitty choice you've ever made."

My heart pinged again.

A tiny crack that had turned into the Grand Canyon of personal choices.

"Go wash your face and come with me."

"Where are we going?"

"I can't tell you."

"You realize that's the theme of my entire life?"

"I'll go inside and talk to the blueberry bush while you pull yourself together."

I rolled my eyes. "Don't."

I started crying again and skipped the bathroom. Instead, I grabbed my purse off the counter and locked the door on my way out. All the simple things you do before your life changes forever.

CHAPTER TWENTY-TWO

Dylan pulled into the gravel parking lot of a squat white cinderblock building. A sign out front advertised cherry pie and turkey with dressing. I couldn't remember the last time I ate. The scent of fried peaches lingered in the air.

A server in a black tee with his wallet chained to his jeans brought a basket of warm rolls and cornbread to the table. Since I left my phone at home, I didn't have anything to fidget with. Eating seemed like a good substitution. I ordered five servings of pinto beans and crumbled cornbread on top in the hopes I'd return to a former version of myself who loved her life as much as food. Fake it 'til you make it.

"He's never on time." Dylan's eyes swept across the empty parking lot.

"Why?"

"I've never asked. I assume it has something to do with doubling back and making sure none of us were followed."

Dylan possessed a natural paranoia that the rest of us had to work at if we wanted to keep up appearances. I assumed Aaron's paranoia sprang from his job.

Across the diner, one of the double glass doors opened, and Aaron stepped inside wearing a faded green windbreaker and aviators.

Slapping hands with Dylan over the table, Aaron left his glasses on. "Thanks for meeting me so far out on such short notice." Aaron's eyes did a sweep of the parking lot, out to the long stretch of highway. "I'll get right to it."

Pulling a plastic bag from the inside of his jacket, Aaron dumped an envelope onto the table. "There are papers in there. Open it up and pull them out."

The level of secrecy turned up a notch.

"Why me?" Dylan asked, slowly.

"Because I cannot have my fingerprints anywhere near what I'm about to show you."

Pushing my bowl of cornbread and beans aside, I noticed Aaron was wearing driving gloves.

Dylan tore the envelope open and pulled out what looked like a copy of a photo.

"Tear that envelope up and flush it down the toilet in the men's room before you leave," Aaron said.

Wadding it up and stuffing it in his pocket, Dylan started to unfold the paper, but our server walked out from behind the counter, headed to our table. Dylan slid it under his forearm.

"What can I get you," he asked, only moderately interested.

Aaron waved him away politely. "We're good."

"You sure?"

"Very sure."

"Whatever you say." Off he went, back to the kitchen.

Dylan glanced at Aaron, waited a few seconds, then unfolded the paper. It took me a few seconds to figure out what I was looking at. A copy of four radar photos, all printed on one page. The first photo was a grainy image of three people standing upright in a loose circle, surrounded by what appeared to be blinding, glowing balls of light.

Aaron pointed at the photo. "I know that's you three. I drove out there and the vehicles are gone, but I know it's you guys. It's the exact coordinates I gave you."

I leaned forward, mesmerized. "What is this?"

"That is a highly-classified document I could be court marshalled for showing you."

Dylan locked eyes with him. "Why are you showing us this?"

"What I'm not showing you is actually more important. That is just four stills from last night. That's all I could get without being caught. Whatever was out there was being tracked on radar for over thirty miles, before it led to you."

"What is it?" I asked.

Aaron inhaled and shrugged. "From what I could see, it just looked like fast-moving balls of dense light. It moved across the desert at speeds I could barely fathom. When it reached the three of you, it hovered, broke into nine separate balls of light, and encircled you." Tapping the piece of paper, he pointed to the next quad. "Like you see in the next still right here."

Dylan glanced at me out of the corner of his eye. It was one thing to have absolutely unexplainable things happen. It was another thing to have someone else show up with proof of absolutely unexplainable things.

"So, you saw a ball of light over our heads?"

"Yes. I was watching it on the screen. Then I watched it break into nine balls and encircle you."

I leaned forward. "What else did you see?"

Aaron looked me in the eye and said, "The balls of light orbit slowly around the people for seven minutes. Then they disappear, *and so do the people.*"

Dylan swallowed. Truth is real, and good, but it's still staggering. "What else did you see?" Dylan asked slowly.

"I know what happened," he said calmly, evenly. "So, where did you end up, exactly?"

Answering that question was like admitting insanity. "Somewhere out in the desert."

Aaron leaned back and smiled at Dylan. "You must be over the moon."

"This one encounter has pretty much validated my entire existence."

Aaron nodded. "I've seen some pretty weird stuff, but this is top of the list."

"Why are you doing this?" I asked.

"Because you deserve to know the truth. Everyone deserves to know the truth. For now, this is as good as I can do. You'll have to go the distance yourselves."

Dylan glanced at the quad of photos one more time. A cult-looking image of people, standing in a triangle, circled by light. Proof of the existence of—*something*. At the very least, it was proof we weren't nuts. At that moment in life, it was a win. Small, but pertinent.

I pointed at a ball of light. "What do you think this is?"

"I think you get to answer that yourself."

Dylan snorted. "Well, that was a dodge if I've ever heard one."

Aaron shrugged in a way that suggested Dylan's opinion didn't sway him from his personal truth.

"What does the military think it is?" I asked, genuinely curious.

Aaron was quiet a moment, lips pulled tight, like when he was a freshman at home plate, about to knock the ball out of the park. "A threat."

Little prickles ran down my forearms. "If meeting us is too complicated, you could pass a message through André."

"He's my significant other, not my personal messenger."

"Sorry." I rolled my eyes, embarrassed. "I wasn't thinking about your relationship."

Aaron scooted to the edge of the booth. "It's okay, Skye. I'm pretty sure your superpower is only thinking about yourself. I'm also pretty sure that's what tormented Trevor for so long."

Slapping Dylan on the shoulder, he whispered, "I was never here," and breezed out the door.

The departure signaled a cue to our server, who returned.

"We'll take the check," I said, before remembering I didn't have cash.

Dylan folded the piece of paper and stuffed it into the pocket of his jeans.

"Trevor is going to freak out when he sees this."

"I bet you're resisting the urge to call a press conference."

"I don't know. Sometimes a simple confirmation of truth means the most. I really don't want anyone outside our group to know about this or the rock."

Amen.

It felt wrong that Trevor wasn't there. Tremendous guilt weighed my body down as we stepped into the dusty parking lot. Even if I hadn't been a total dick about the truth, he'd still have to be at work.

Or maybe not.

That summed up my entire life.

Maybe.

Maybe not.

I exhaled, trying to force indecision out of my body, where it would be subject to the laws of gravity. All that indecision would have to crawl along on the top of the jagged rocks like a scorpion. Everyone would run away from it. Compulsively.

Especially me.

If I could just get it out.

Indecision *liked* me.

It had moved into a spare room in my head and taken root without paying rent a long time ago.

Me and indecision.

Indecision and me.

Shifting my eyes, I tried to block the light. The sun was too bright and followed me everywhere.

Another paradox.

I'd been looking for the light my entire life. Then, when I found it, I ducked into a dark room and laid waste to my chiseled plans.

We all did it.

At one time or another.

But I did it compulsively, like an indecision addict.

Dylan was too high on radar images to notice.

This series of events cracked me open. Pieces of my soul floated in my bloodstream. I could feel it. All that indecision evaporated the glue that held my molecules together. Like a candle wick extinguished, I felt that *sizzle*, that sting.

I should have never told Trevor the truth.

Even if it haunted me forever.

Which it did.

Which was why I told him.

Hello, indecision.

It's nice to see you again.

Dylan paced. The soft *whomp* of his Chuck Taylors served as a beacon.

"This," he said. "This is incredible."

An incredible mess.

"Do you know what this means?"

"That we're not totally crazy?"

Dylan stopped in front of me, face pinched. "No. Stop struggling with sanity. Sanity does not hold value, except that which society puts on normal. Normal people don't go out in the desert looking for magnificence."

He had me there.

Normal people do not lose time or mass hallucinate.

"Every extraordinary thing ever done by humans was considered crazy at the time."

Dylan's ability to make crazy seem logical was unprecedented.

"True."

"This is it," he said emphatically.

"What is 'it'?"

"That's the very last piece of the puzzle."

"Have you been putting all the pieces together?" I was genuinely curious, because I had no idea if our puzzle looked like a princess castle, or a post-apocalyptic wasteland.

"Don't be daft, Skye."

"But we don't know what the light is."

"Sure, we do. It's intelligence. It's photons, charged particles burning through our atmosphere. It's an emanation. A reflection, possibly. Like a coded message, sent through space. A memo from the cosmos."

"A text from God."

Dylan snapped his fingers so fast and so loud it made me jump. "Exactly," he said, suddenly excited.

While I loved his enthusiasm, I didn't always follow. The sun, the exhaustion, the strange feeling I hadn't slept in years held me in suspended animation. "Exactly what?"

"That's what we have to figure out."

"I'm tired of the riddles, Dylan. I want clear sentences, full of perfect grammar. I'm tired of stumbling from one vague clue to the next, and acting like it's the most amazing thing to ever be held up on planet Earth."

He flipped his sunglasses up to his forehead and glared. "Why are you such a brat?"

"What? We can't figure out what this means, and suddenly I'm the selfish asshole?"

"It doesn't matter whether you figure out the meaning or not. You're still the selfish asshole."

A harsh sting quivered in my body. I could not believe he'd said that. Not Dylan. I felt judged and defeated by the entire world.

And angry.

"I cannot believe you just said that."

"Look, I'm not trying to be a dick. I love you regardless of where you fall on the selfish spectrum, but it creates a ton of problems. You didn't tell Trevor that you knew that guy before you left because you wanted to heal and fix your relationship. You told him because you felt bad and wanted to absolve yourself of that sin. Look, I get it. I'm not living by myself because I'm easy to deal with. I'm a total pain. But you, princess, have to reach a point where the entire world isn't required to be your on-call everything."

I'd been crying off and on all day, making up for years of stoic perseverance. I hated crying. Drowning had to be easier to deal with than crying. To top it off, the only person I'd ever truly felt was playing Team Skye just threw his bat on the ground.

"I told Trevor because I thought he should know the truth."

"You told Trevor because your heart is heavy."

"You're supposed to be on my side."

"I am. No one else talks to you like this."

"You're wrong. Everyone talks to me like this, especially Stella."

"Then take this as a sign, and change."

Two old trucks slowed on the highway and turned into the empty lot.

"Come on, let's go," Dylan said. "I've got to drop you off at home and go tell Trevor."

CHAPTER TWENTY-THREE

T wo police cars were parked in front of the house when Dylan turned onto my street. Cops never bothered him, so he didn't sink down in his seat and suggest shady shit like driving by without stopping.

I knew exactly what happened. The ugh in my soul was real. My sister had kicked Ethan's ass. Probably at the airport, maybe even in the car. My vote went toward the car, because my sister could really throw a punch in a tight space.

Dylan pulled into the driveway behind my Honda. "What's up with Las Cruces' finest?"

Glancing back over my shoulder, I said, "I think my sister was a Hell's Angel in a past life."

An officer stepped out of one of the patrol cars. A man. From the other car, a woman.

"I'll wait here," Dylan said, "just in case."

I glanced over at his golden tan, his blue eyes flickering under his worn but stylish aviators. Sweat trickled down his temple. A rugged, manly sweat that would make Jack London proud.

"Yeah, okay," I said. "Thanks."

And I stepped out of his truck.

And changed forever.

In the afternoon glare I shielded my eyes.

"I'm Officer Gibbs," the man said.

"I'm Officer Riley," the woman said. "Are you Skye?"

"What's this about?"

"Can we talk to you inside?"

I paused. It was the first time in my life I could feel the planet moving. *Whoosh.* Somewhere far away in South Carolina, the ocean sloshed against the shores. A few beetle carcasses lay in the rock garden next to a gnome. I could feel the sky touching the top of my head. I could feel everything.

"Is this about my sister?"

Officer Gibbs nodded.

"Who's in the truck?" Officer Riley asked.

"My best friend."

"Tell him to come in with you."

"We can post bail," I said.

"Let's go in and talk about it," Officer Gibbs said.

The cool, dim hall was like entering a dark chamber of the underworld after the summer heat. My eyes were still adjusting to the change when Officer Gibbs said, "Stella was in an accident."

"What? You mean she hit him by accident?"

"No. He hit her."

"What? Ethan hit her? That's ludicrous, and totally out of character."

"His name isn't Ethan."

"What are you talking about?"

"There was an accident on the road. Your sister stopped to help. She was struck by a motorist."

"What do you mean, struck by a motorist?"

"Someone lost control of their vehicle and hit her."

The door opened behind us, flooding the hall with light.

"Well, where is she?"

"She—," Officer Gibbs hesitated.

Entire universes were born in that pause. It was that long. I felt the blood in my veins. My heartbeat palpitated.

"She didn't make it."

Behind me, Dylan made this quick inhalation, a sound I'd never heard. A sharp intake of breath. A sound I'd never forget.

"I don't understand."

Officer Riley took a deep breath. "She died on the way to the hospital."

I could be a difficult and complicated girl, but I was confused. "She can't be dead. Her clothes are right there."

Officer Gibbs looked down the hall at Stella's dirty clothes strewn across the floor. A thong. A dark blue tee. A camo tank. A pair of jeans.

Officer Gibbs laid his hand on my shoulder. "I'm very sorry."

"About what?"

It was like I was in a long, underground tunnel, and a voice on a loudspeaker was telling us the world was ending. Absolutely nothing made sense.

"I'm sorry. I was the first officer on the scene."

"And you checked her for a pulse?"

His lips pinched up in that sad way adults do when they're talking to little kids and don't want to admit the truth. His bottom lip trembled, and a wave of dread slammed into me unlike anything I'd ever felt. From where I was standing, I could see Dryer Bunny propped up on her bed. Stella's favorite childhood bunny I'd shoved in the dryer when I was three. Its matted fur and melted whiskers never bothered Stella. She just kept on loving Dryer Bunny.

"Oh, my God," Dylan said, and sat down on the floor.

That's a good idea, I thought. Standing up was hard. Growing up was hard.

The next thing I knew, I heard my forearms slapping against the tile. A second later, I was totally out.

Those precious few seconds between waking and opening my eyes held me in limbo. I didn't know where I was. A blissful ignorance. I wasn't sure how long I could make it last. The scene in the hallway flooded my brain, and I cracked one eye open.

Dylan was laying sideways in a chair with his head against the windowsill. A soft light glowed over the bed.

Disoriented beyond belief, I rolled over and whispered, "Where are we?"

Dylan shot straight up in the chair, stunned. "What?"

"Where are we?"

"Los Cruces Regional."

My eyes swept around the room. "When did hospital rooms start looking like hotel rooms?"

He rubbed his face vigorously and looked like a cartoon character. "I don't know. These places give me the creeps."

"Why are we here?"

"You. Why are *you* here? Because, apparently, when you lose consciousness in front of a police officer, they can't just step over you and walk away. It becomes a liability for the police department."

His eyes were so red.

"Did that thing in the hallway really happen?"

He stopped squirming in his chair and made eye contact.

I mouthed the word, "How?"

"It was just Stella being Stella. She pulled over to help someone. Some idiot who'd just come from renewing his driver's license ran into her."

I brought my hands to my face to hide from the whole thing, except I'd been hiding for so long. Running and hiding. "This is all my fault. I should have never let her drive Ethan."

"I get that your superpower is making everything about you, but Stella was on that two-lane road that leads out of the city. No one knows where she was going."

"No," I shook my head.

"Yes."

"How can you look for meaning in everything except this? How? Seriously. Tell me that."

"Don't get weird with me. I'm in just as much shock as you are."

My lips quivered, and I was afraid I wouldn't be able to talk. "Where are my parents?"

"I called them. They were at the funeral home the last time I talked to them."

It was the most awful answer in the world.

"Where's Buck?"

"With Trevor. Hopefully they're heating up that fifty count Bagel Minis I bought yesterday."

"Did he say anything about me?"

"I won't go into the expletives, but he's pretty mad."

I stared at the ceiling. "This is all so unbelievably fucked up."

Dylan nodded, pulling the extra blanket from the end of the bed and throwing it over his shoulders. Tears backed up in his eyes. "This is hard," he said.

"It's not real," I blurted out spit and desperation. "We're going to wake up. We were out in the desert, and something moved us. Something moved us. This isn't really happening."

"It's what the lights were trying to tell us."

"*What? No. No, Dylan.* You said the lights were going to help us make sense of our lives."

His chin dropped down and I couldn't see the tears running down his cheeks, but I could hear them. Like an awful dam busting loose. Like a terrible flood of angels descending on the Earth. "When the wreckage is cleared, I think we might see this for what it is."

"And what is that?"

"You're pinning me against the wall, Skye." He inhaled sharply in the small room, taking some of my next breath.

I huffed and I puffed to bring my sister back. "I want her here," I said, so urgently it scared me.

"She is. She's downstairs. In the morgue."

He slayed me with one response. I spent the next four hours crying, and he never left my side, never unclenched my hand, never looked away from my spit sobbing drooling uncontrollable crying.

Best friends aren't a simple declaration with necklaces and emojis. They are carved from the very existence of our lives. They are forged like steel from swords of old. They are hand-woven into a mysterious fabric constructed of the humming strings that make up the universe.

"I should have driven Ethan to the airport," I blubbered.

"It wouldn't have mattered, Skye. You wouldn't have been on that road leading out of town. No one even knows where she was going."

"But maybe, if there was one more car on the road, it would have changed the entire dynamic, and that one car wouldn't have been there. It would have been one street over," I said, reaching for any logic I could get my hands on.

"You're trying to make sense of this by going backwards. Stop. This is how you got stuck in that fucking loop for six years. We're going to make sense of this going forward, and it's going to hurt. It was always going to hurt."

CHAPTER TWENTY-FOUR

The main room of Paley Brothers Funeral Home was quiet. Black and beige curtains hung along the edges of the room. Stella was up at the very front, surrounded by magnificent pink roses and cops in uniform. I'd never seen so many cops in one place. Everyone my sister knew had the power to arrest me. Black uniforms reflected across the sheen of her closed ivory coffin. It was altogether terrible. I'd come from the hospital where I was discharged. The silence of the hospital made me antsy. The silence of the funeral home was too much. I saw now the quiet places weren't for cups of tea and yoga. Quiet places ushered death over the face of a planet I'd been running across my entire adult life.

Dylan walked through the sea of strangers. He laid his hands on either side of the podium and looked out at us. It took a minute, but finally he dropped his head and said, "'I'd rather be a superb meteor, every atom of me in magnificent glow, than a sleepy permanent planet. The function of man is to live. I shall not waste my days trying to prolong them. I shall use my time.' Jack London, but it sums up Stella well."

He held tight to the podium, dressed in wrinkled flannel, with a five o'clock shadow, looking like London himself had just stumbled from a rocky trail into a funeral service.

Slumped halfway down in my seat, I clutched Dryer Bunny and stared at my hospital wristband to keep from crying in front of all these people I'd never met. Dryer Bunny stared up at me with his one blue eye and matted fur. His melted whiskers had once been straight lines, like my life. I just couldn't get my existence to right itself. I dangled from a burnt thread over a dark abyss. The darkest Freudian analysis didn't touch the awful reality of sitting in a strange chair, in a strange room, saying goodbye.

I wanted desperately to go back to a time when my biggest concern in life was saving up my allowance to drive Dad's car out to the mall and buy more Juicy Tubes. I believed they made me more kissable. It never ever occurred to me that Trevor kissed me because he loved me. I thought it was because I was wet and fruity.

Currently sitting two rows back, he hadn't spoken to me. All I got was a pinched smile when he walked into the funeral home, a half-wave that was obligatory. I wanted to go back to the mall and stop the free fall.

Dylan thrust his chin out and tilted his head back. Pointing to a scar almost impossible to see unless you were underneath him looking through a microscope, he said,

"This is from the day I met Stella. She let a wooden gate close in my face."

Dad chuckled, smooth and easy, but I could tell he was seconds from crying. I'd been bursting into tears ever since I came home and found the cops in the front yard.

Buck howled outside. Parked in the shade, he relaxed on the love seat with a big bowl of water. The rest of us were scorched inside and didn't have Dylan's amazing dog karma.

"Stella wasn't like me," Dylan said. "She didn't find meaning in the late afternoon sun illuminating the passage I just recited. But I did. Accepting people exactly as they are lies in the ability to resist the urge to convince them to be just like you. Most people are carbon copies. Stella was an original."

Dylan paused, eyes slick with sadness. He looked out at all of us. The survivors. Stella was the general who led us through war. Once we were safely on the other side, she said goodbye.

There are lots of glib sayings. Time will heal. Life goes on. It's all bullshit. A single phrase repeated in my head like a scratched CD:

I miss you.
Sisters are the silent spaces in between heartbeats.

I miss you.
Always present tense.

I miss you.

A mantra.

A holy hippie harmony bowl of heavenly weight.

Like the stars were so sad they had to rest on my shoulders.

A preprogrammed code.

A reminder.

A memo.

A note that sent me right back to *I miss you*, regardless of how far away I tried to go. And, trust me, I wanted desperately to go back. I wanted to go back to the old days when I could lie to myself, but I'd spent the entire summer having my lies taken away, like a screaming toddler in full meltdown. Lies had been a slippery slope into oblivion. I'd invested too much energy in letting go. Even Trevor, two rows back. I'd gone away, but never let him go. I couldn't turn back. There is a place pinched tight between the extremes of pleasure and the scorch of pain where I didn't grow up, but instead crossed over into the age of abandon.

There, in my fold-up chair, in a plain room, with no ferryman demanding a coin, I passed into a new age. Not an actual age, like eighteen or twenty-five or thirty-nine, but a place in myself where I knew if I didn't let go, I'd be dragged backwards, from shore to deep sea.

Buck howled again.

I sat upright, startled, deep in grief, crying, trying to inhale, keep the air flowing in my lungs. Trying not to be a drama queen and faint. The cop next to me reached for my hand. He squeezed, and I closed my eyes for a second, but couldn't breathe.

Dylan's face pinched in agony. "Stella never let me win. Not at chess or darts or horseshoes. Sometimes, I won on my own. I was a champion, out there in the setting sun. I'd beat the girl who'd kicked my ass from the day we met. It didn't happen often, but it happened. Occasionally. She was always so alive. It's just hard to imagine a world without her." And with that admission, he gave an abrupt bow, and stepped away from the podium in tears.

The sharp edge of reality would have slayed us all, but the door to the funeral home banged against the wall. We turned, shocked and startled, to see Wormy standing in the doorway. Clutching a bottle of Stoli, she stumbled forward, about as drunk as a person could be. So drunk I could smell the shots from my seat. I hated her. I thought I hated her for Trevor, but ruining my sister's funeral was more than hate, it was unforgivable.

"You can have Trevor, bitch, but get out of my sister's funeral," I turned around in my seat and screamed.

My mother gasped so loud I could hear her over everyone talking at once.

Trevor stood quickly to usher his train wreck wife out to the parking lot.

Dylan said, "What the *actual* fuck?"

Daddy started crying.

My beautiful mother pushed her way into the aisle.

A wave of cops walked in her direction, but I stumbled out of my seat holding onto Dryer Bunny. I pushed through the crowd to punch Wormy in the face. I didn't care if the entire room was wall to wall with cops. If my sister could punch out her ex, then surely, I could join the club and punch Wormy. Punch her for being where I'd wanted to be, and carelessly throwing it all away. Punch her for calling me Cutesy Girl in high school. Punch her because I was so angry with the world that violence felt like the answer.

And I would have.

Punched her lights out.

In front of three dozen cops.

Knocked her clear to Kingdom Come.

But Trevor reached her first, grabbing her arm. Wormy pulled away with such force that she fell into a row of chairs. Trevor grabbed her again, yanking her upright. Wormy pulled her fist back, and I thought she was going to deck him, but instead, she screamed, "I loved her."

All slurred together.

But we all heard it.

I stood there like a lunatic, trying to figure out why that awful girl was crashing my sister's funeral, when my eyes darted to Trevor. It was like I could read his mind. In that instant, the truth descended on me like Moses coming down from the mountain. Wormy wasn't cheating on Trevor with some guy. Wormy was leaving him *for my sister*. OMG. *THIS* was the thing Stella kept circling around. Of all the convoluted truths I'd ever concealed from myself, this was the prize winner.

Trevor's brow pinched tight.

My dad's mouth fell open.

Slumped and weary, Wormy fell forward. The wrinkles around her eyes dry riverbeds of regret. "We think we're so smart," she slurred, "with our phones and satellites and microscopes, but we don't know why we dream. And we don't know why we die. And we don't know why we love. And I loved her." The bottle of Stoli hit the floor upright.

Then she vomited all over the black and gold diamond carpet.

My mom gasped and ran forward. "Someone help her."

I stood there, marveling over the fact that it had been Stella and Wormy sitting in a tree, and I'd never seen it. Not once. My sister was silent like ninja.

Buck walked through the open door.

The sight of that old dog wagging his tail was enough to send me over the edge.

Because that was exactly where I'd been going since I returned.

Over the edge.

Over the edge.

I looked around the room at people I didn't know sitting on pews, at the funeral of a sister I clearly didn't know. An employee of the funeral home swooped in with paper towels and spray cleaner. Wormy's breath was raspy and even, like she was holding on for dear life. Two officers reached for her arm, but she waved them away.

Over the edge.

Her fingers reached for the chair. The entire world distilled into the glowing white tip of her index finger, squeezing tight.

Over the edge.

Maybe Trevor had already gone over the edge and was waiting to catch me when I hit bottom.

Which would be any minute now.

Or just maybe I was going to have to catch myself. A self-catching princess.

No one stays in free fall forever.

It just feels that way.

Wormy inhaled deep, and I thought she was going to rise from the fold-up chair like a mighty Titan, but instead, she lifted her eyes to me, and only slightly. The glistening tears reflected a single beam of light streaming in from a skylight.

For a split second, her tears created champagne rainbows dancing over her red cheeks.

Salt water and light.

The ingredients of life.

I felt a hand slip into mine. In a weird dreamlike state I was pulled upright. Dylan and I walked out the doors.

An hour later Joshua trees came into view on the horizon. The place of my youth. A full circle loop from past to present. A place of singing sand dunes and carpets of wildflowers. A place of ancient people who carved deep into the earth. The place we all end up.

"Did you know?" I ask, laying my palms flat on my knees, braced for the answer.

Dylan shook his head, exhaled. "No." His hands dropped to the bottom of the steering wheel. "But I guess I should have."

"This is why Stella kept asking me about Trevor. She knew. I thought she was just being a dick and pointing out past failures. Instead, she knew her and Wormy wanted to jump ship. If Trevor and I were together then it made for a smooth transition."

"Yeah," he said quietly, "with you back in town it created an easy out."

An easy out. The theme of my life.

I covered my face with my hands because keeping my eyes open was overwhelming. "What are you doing with that rock?"

"Getting to know each other."

"Don't you want to know what it is?"

"I know what it is. It's space debris. If I go and try to find more info I just end up with a bunch of uptight academics demanding I hand it over." Wagging a finger in my direction he says, "That is Dylan's rock."

Serious, emphatic tones always made me laugh. "Fair enough."

"Finders, keepers."

"Losers, weepers."

Without even thinking we did a fist bump.

"If Stella had told me about Wormy I never would have told Trevor the truth."

"Which means you'd always be a dirtbag."

I rolled my eyes letting them come to rest in full stink mode. "Uncomplicated. It would have uncomplicated the situation."

"I love you but you're dreaming. Nothing and I do mean *nothing* uncomplicates this situation."

"Do you think she just didn't trust me?"

"I think Stella always erred on the side of caution. Rightfully so. I think she wanted something and we put her on a pedestal. She wanted something and angled to get it in the most uncomplicated way. I think she didn't want to be a homewrecker and then poof you showed up. If you hooked up with Trevor it untangled a tangly situation."

"Is that a word? *Tangly?*"

He shrugged. "I'm just saying."

"My sister. The schemer."

"We're all scheming down here on planet Earth. I see now that Stella was my twin. Same flaws. Same strengths."

Turning the wheel, he took a dirt road leading off the two-lane road. We bumped across the earth packed hard with the bones of all the choices that came before us.

"Do you think Trevor will ever forgive me?"

"Probably not. I don't know. But I'm fully back on the market and I have my own space debris," he winked.

I looked over at his red eyes. Even though he'd been crying the way his hair tumbled over his forehead still signaled he was emotional miles ahead of me. Land and sky stretched out in front of the truck. All of that wide open space made my heart race. Like freedom was a prison, an optical illusion. It didn't matter if I could escape because I'd never get anywhere. I'd careen across the open expanse forever, never arriving, never departing. Just constantly running away from invisible things that were everywhere.

Exhausted and hungry, blinded and somehow cold with the wind on my arms, I rolled up the window and leaned back, letting my head bump against the plastic headrest.

Dust burned my nostrils, but I liked the feeling of my head bumping. A feeling of surrender. Bump me along, dear universe, I thought. Dylan inhaled, grinding gears. I kept my eyes closed, thinking that if I couldn't see where I was going then eventually, I'd forget where I'd been. A sweet amnesia of surrender from the passenger seat of a truck with its bumper held on by bungee cords and duct tape. We drove like that into the dawn. Greasy and sweaty and falling apart we arrived in the high desert with cups of gas station coffee in our hands.

The sharp grind of downshifting made me focus. There in front of us were the famous wild asses of the Mojave Desert. Donkeys to the less experienced. Herds of wild asses were legendary. I'd never actually seen a herd.

Dylan slowed to a roll. From the window I could see their furry faces and twitchy ears. All of them turned to face us. Hundreds, some still munching on dry grass and shrubs.

"Look," Dylan whispered.

Several wild asses cocked their heads and swished tails.

There they were, free and together. Maybe not the perfect set up. Finding food and water out in the desert was no small task. But out under that blue sky they possessed a sense of togetherness I'd lost. Misplaced years before, when I'd run out on Trevor because I was too afraid to run with my herd.

Dylan slowed to a complete stop and opened his creaky door. Several wild asses snorted and backed up. Dylan stopped, hand still on the door handle.

"Have you ever seen them before?" I whispered.

"Not this close."

"They're amazing."

"I've got some food. Jump into the truck bed with me," he said, slipping out of the cab and running to the back.

More snorts and a few ear twitches, but no one moved so I slipped out quietly and swiftly, hoisting myself into the truck bed.

"Why do you have all this bread and peanut butter?"

Dylan waved away my silliness. "I was distressed, and they were having a sale."

Out there I saw the juxtaposition so clearly. Life and death in an endless circle. One feeding the other. We bookend death with life, but it's not that simple. If life is the beginning, and death is the end, then what is all the in-between?

It's the nature of reality.

In that single instant, I saw it as individual and clear as a snowflake, as unique as a fingerprint. A dynamic network of choices, connecting to choices, that hook to people and group together to form a pattern of destiny.

The mystery was formed by the choices.

What you hold onto.

What you let go of.

What you let hold onto you.

CHAPTER TWENTY-FIVE

Daddy found me outside the B&B, laying on the ground under a sprawling tree. It was a magnificent tree, with pebbles surrounding the base, next to a cool fountain. Flat on my back, eyes closed, I listened to streams of little pink heart garland and paper blossoms flutter in the slight breeze. Lavender and basil, in huge terra cotta pots spaced throughout the grounds, scented the air. It was beautiful, and made me want to cry.

I heard Daddy's footsteps but didn't move.

Kneeling at my side, he whispered. "You alright?"

Without opening my eyes, I asked, "Are you?"

"No. But I'm getting married, and I want to be a whole, functioning person for the woman I love."

I shielded my eyes from the sun and cracked one open. "How do you do that?"

"Do what?"

"Remain whole when the world collapses?"

"It's my superpower."

"I wish it was genetic."

Resting a knee on the ground, he asked, "What are you doing out here?"

"Practicing Ho'oponopono."

"Well," he said slowly, "that's interesting."

"The psychic said it would help ground me and bring clarity."

"Ahh, yes. Stella told me about him."

Hearing her name was like the sharp cry of a lost animal. I sat upright, blood rushing to my head, making me dizzy. "Do you think she's here?"

"I think we want her to be here."

New tears pushed into my eyes. Thoughts of mascara running down my cheeks held them back. Shallow and superficial have their place. "Do you think this was meant to happen?"

"I think you're asking the wrong question. I think everyone on this planet has a timer. And when the timer dings, your time is up."

Sitting on the ground under a tree, I sucked back my tears, but I couldn't make them stop. "Why do you think she didn't tell us about Wormy?"

"Because Trevor was involved, and you came back suddenly. I think that complicated it all. Trevor likes you. Wormy likes her. Divorce is messy, honey."

"But she—,"

"Listen," Daddy took my hand and squeezed tight. "I'm going to tell you a story. This is what we have to do to get past all of this. We have to find a tiny crumb, just one, and plant it like a seed."

Tears fell from my eyes, and I started bawling like a three-year-old. It was Stella's favorite story. *Crumb.* Daddy had been telling it my entire life.

Inhaling sharply, he continued, "Water it with a thousand pulsing stars. Give it room to grow, but stay near. Crumbs do not like to be left alone. When you're sleeping, dream it grows. Watch that crumb grow into a vine, growing forward. 'It's only a crumb', some will say, derisively. Ignore those people. Crumbs have no use for haters. Talk to your crumb. At first, it will be so tiny. Say things like, 'Listen up, crumb. It's you and me, we're in this together. Grow big and tall, and one day you won't be a crumb at all.'"

My chin quivered. He'd told it millions of times. "Tell that crumb story," Stella yelled, eight years old, dressed in snow boots and a pink tutu. I stared at my daddy like he was the only thing on the planet. Like my entire existence wrapped around that moment.

Daddy whispered, "Some people will say, 'That dumb crumb will never grow.' Their hearts are black. Don't waste your time forgiving those people. Keep your eyes on your crumb, give it room to grow, sunlight, moonlight, and a magical toad."

"This whole thing has reduced me to a single speck on the blip of the universe, and it scares me, and I'm worried I won't survive this," I said. It was true. Hopelessly dramatic, but exactly how I felt. "What if I can't find a crumb?"

"The most beautiful stories always start with wreckage." Dylan said, somewhere behind the tree.

"Fucking Jack. Like seriously, how did he know?"

Dylan walked into view wearing the exact same pair of jeans from the funeral. "Because, when you hang around out in the wild, you have to have something to show for it."

I'd avoided stories about desperate survival, freezing to death, watching the world collapse in surrender, my entire life. I was too neurotic and desperate to look deep into the odds. Dylan loved odds. Not me. He was the dice thrower. I was the girl who sat on the edge of the world and watched it burn. Life was a dance on top of a roulette table, on top of a celestial fire that spun around and around on the edge of destiny. The cosmic gamble. I was too shell-shocked to embrace chaos like a long-lost cousin.

Daddy pulled a real but pained smile. "Come on," he said, "the ceremony is about to begin."

I pushed off the ground, palms covered in dust.

Dust to dust.

Gotta find my crumb.

Dang.

It was 9 AM, and already the longest day of my life.

Dylan was waiting for me in the kitchen off the main room. Too hot to hold the ceremony outside, I walked around the air-conditioned B&B, sweaty, dusty, with little pieces of dried grass stuck to my clothes.

He picked a tiny leaf out of my hair. "You need to stop obsessing."

"I'm not obsessing. I'm processing."

"You're thinking about all the years you spent out east with some hipster douchebag who drove a nice car, when you could have been here, with your sister."

Smacking my palms against my thighs, trying to get rid of dusty patches, I glared at him. "You say that like it's a bad thing."

"Look, Stella was an awesome piece of work. I loved sitting out in the desert, drinking Miller High Life, listening to the coyotes howl, playing charades in the firelight."

"You played charades with my sister?"

"Sure. Isn't that what you were doing back east? Playing charades? *Sounds like? Feels like? Rhymes with?*"

"You saying those six years were nothing more than a game?"

"We were all playing the same game in different places on the board. Even Trevor was playing. It's okay to admit the truth, even if it's hard." Shoving his hands into the pockets of his jeans, he pinched his lips tight, then said, "None of us had a future with Stella."

"You're saying this was meant to happen?"

"I'm saying everything has meaning."

"Which you can't prove."

"Which is cool." He half-smiled and shrugged. "Because you can't prove everything is random."

The minister poked her head around the corner. "We're ready to begin now."

Dylan reached for my hand. "Won't you join me for the rest of our lives?"

My mom cried all the way down the narrow aisle. So did Daddy. I sat next to Dylan, obsessing over how we buried my sister one day, married my parents the next. There's a pain that comes over you when someone dies that must feel a lot like freezing to death. Slow, horrific, *inevitable*. Light cascaded through the tall windows, a pale color that illuminated, but didn't burn. I suspected the burn came later, or that I was so emotionally defunct that it wouldn't come at all.

I had an incredible urge to pull out my phone and find old Juicy Tubes on eBay. Not because they'd be fresh enough to use; I just wanted to carry them around in the bottom of my purse like a security blanket. A reminder that life could be simple again. I sighed, trying to push back against my lunacy, but only ended up crying. Dylan reached over, slipping his arm around my shoulder. My white fold-out chair tipped as I leaned into him.

"I'm sorry," I blubbered. Spit and tears wove into all my expressions.

"You're not alone," he whispered.

I lifted my eyes, and, through a wall of salt water, I said, "Neither are you."

"Everything we are given returns to its original source," the minister said.

My parents were up there on the polished wood floor, renewing a love that crossed a lifetime. That was their gift to us. Now it was a gift to me. My other half was gone. Maybe I loved Stella more than she loved me. Maybe she loved me more. Isn't that how it is, sometimes? One loving the other just a teeny bit more, so it tips the scale. You're just staring across the fire pit at someone, ears buzzing from one too many High Life's, and you contemplate, for the briefest of seconds, what it would be like to be their everything.

Dylan squeezed my shoulder. Stella loved Lip Smackers.

I had moments where I swore adjusting my belt buckle would align my entire life. I thought the strange stillness that came to pass was a new invitation to speak. I stumbled backwards into these thoughts with the knowledge that I couldn't build a future based on a moment I'd been recycling for years.

Mom and dad were at the front of the room, holding hands, smiling, crying. The rest of the room filled with friends.

Stella used to kick her boots up on the patio furniture and say, "One day, we'll all be old, or one day we'll all be dead. Either way, live accordingly." Then she'd nod, tip her beer, and when the fire popped, it felt like falling in love. My sister was the wisest person I'd ever known. The people who don't give two shits about wisdom are the ones who find it first. She was my constant through everything. Now my constant was gone. I wanted to be able to say something dignified, but honestly, if someone kicks you in the balls, the last thing you want to do is stand around pontificating about it.

I inhaled deeply.

I selfishly wanted Trevor to walk in and take a seat next to me.

Elementary particles danced in the pale light.

"Let's all hold hands and say a prayer," the minister said.

I realized I hadn't heard a word of my parents' vows. Not a sentence or a phrase. I'd been swimming in my own loss too much to hear life-affirming words of love.

Story of my life.

Daddy was a train wreck.

Mom was beautiful and sad.

A room full of whispered condolences and sturdy handshakes of congratulations. Mom looked like Marlene

Dietrich in her ivory white satin dress, tears staining the bodice in a Rorschach pattern recorded deep into the psyche of our lives.

People poured into the aisle, and I realized the ceremony was over.

The guy Dylan sold the bull semen to was at the buffet table.

"What are you doing?" I asked casually, genuinely curious.

He pointed at Daddy. "I've known your father since we were nine years old."

"Huh," Dylan said over my shoulder, "small world."

I ate my herbed goat cheese on a baguette slice and thought about the nature of reality. I'd been thinking about it since that first night at Dylan's, when my sister said she had to write a paper. Zen koans, misfires, false starts, sure things, and my redneck mystic sister.

William James believed we create the truths we register.

My favorite fortune, the one stuffed secretly in my wallet, read: *It does not matter how slowly you go, as long as you do not stop.*

I was about to excuse myself to start writing it all down. I needed to compose this time in our lives. I had this obsessive idea that the nature of reality would make sense if I could just get it down on paper.

A man in a sports jacket approached me and touched my elbow. "I know this is an awkward time, but I really need to talk to you."

CHAPTER TWENTY-SIX

Three weeks after the funeral/wedding, I stood in the carport, staring down into my trunk. Empty squares on a calendar showed the summer coming to a close, and the suffocating heat finally lifted. The tunnel system was still intact, along with all the structures, but Mouse City was strangely empty.

I heard Dylan's truck take the corner at the end of my street. He whipped into the driveway behind me like he was afraid I'd try to escape. Truthfully, I'd had enough escape for a while. Escape had worn me out. I'd been doing it for close to a decade. What I really wanted to do was just stand right there and build something. Even if it was with LEGOs or playing cards instead of concrete and steel.

On that random Thursday afternoon, I'd gone outside to find inspiration, but instead found the mice missing.

Dylan flashed a smile, tossing his blonde bangs off his forehead. "Hey, princess. Are we cool?"

For weeks he'd been picking the lock on the kitchen door and sneaking inside. I hid in the guest room and refused to come out. Dylan propped himself up next to Buck in the hall and read aloud from a Jack London collection, while I clutched Dryer Bunny on the other side of the door and cried. It made sense at the time.

From the shade of the carport I saw him perfectly. The deep blue of his eyes held the mystery of pain, but only I would notice. For all the world he was fine. Hair too long, clothes too wrinkled, Buck at his side.

"Are you asking if I forgive you for picking my locks and heckling me in the name of mental health?"

"Sure." He stopped in the sunlight at the edge of the carport. "That's one way to put it."

"Yes," I sighed. "Breaking and entering is a forgivable offense when you're worried."

"I was counting on sanity to prevail. What are you doing out here?"

I gestured to my trunk. "The mice left."

Dylan furrowed his brow. "Huh. Let me see."

I stepped aside and he joined me. We both stared down at the remnants of a once flourishing habitat.

"It's symbolic." I felt all the more depressed for having said it out loud.

Dylan glanced at me out of the corner of his eye. "How so?"

"I mean, even the mice don't like me enough to hang around and watch my moping."

"Doubtful." He peered into a tiny house-like thing made from a wicker purse.

"You don't think the rodents have abandoned me?"

"Well, I think they left, but not for the reasons you're going on about."

"Uh huh. Are you trying to make me feel better?"

"Not at all. Listen, haven't you heard of John Calhoun?"

"No."

"He was an ethologist. He did a bunch of experiments back in the '50s. He picked mice. He wanted to create Utopia. He gave the mice a perfect setup. No stress, no one there to eat them, abundant food, safety. In general, an awesome place for mice to live. Then, he kicked up his heels on the corner of his desk and waited for the bliss of Utopia. Which never came. You can look it up, but it amounts to this: there were four stages to Mouse Utopia: Strive. Exploit. Equilibrium. Extinction. He thought the mice would settle into a perfect world if they had everything they needed. Instead, they became violent and obsessively groomed and lost interest in raising their children. They withdrew, and social structure broke down."

"Is that supposed to cheer me up?"

"I'm trying to tell you that the mammalian brain isn't structured to live in paradise. It's structured to strive and fuck up and train wreck and correct course. Even the mice knew that. So, even though the mice had paradise by the dashboard light, they struck out on their own and, by doing so, they ensured their future success. In short, your mice are smart, and will not go down the mouse hole of extinction."

"Are you flirting with me?"

Dylan smiled, "No, I'm trying to tell you that by leaving six years ago, you upset the equilibrium, and maybe that was a good thing. Not in every way, but in some important ways. Maybe running is coded so deep into our experience that we have to run. At least a few times. You left, and that destroyed the natural order, but now you're back, and order has reasserted itself."

"So, you think the mice don't hate me?"

"I think you and the mice are one."

"A weird Aesop's Fables with rodents."

"Or maybe it's what Jack was trying to tell us about accepting the call of the wild: Stay out too long in the wild, you die. Stay in too long, and you die. Life, equilibrium, and balance is a dance we do all day. Everyone thinks balance is static. Balance is growth. Balance is that train speeding down the track, a hundred million miles per hour, on a great rotating ball, and staying upright."

Pulling something from his pocket he held it out to me. A small plastic racing car guy from a Japanese anime.

"What is that?"

"When our house was destroyed by Katrina my dad and I went to North Alabama to ride it out. Once the flood waters receded we went back. That thing you're holding was a key chain I'd kept on top of my dresser. It was the only thing left. Wedged in-between some bricks I pulled it out. Then my dad and I moved here. That little Japanese race car driver was all I had to rebuild. You hold onto him for awhile. He's a crafty little dude."

Inside, Dylan leafed through stacks of papers on the kitchen table. "What have you been doing?"

"I wrote Stella's paper on the Nature of Reality, typed it up, and turned it in to her professor. He probably thinks I'm a looney, but I don't care."

"Wow. This is deep. You wrote all of this out on paper? This is like the entire summer. So, what's your final conclusion?"

"That I'm selfish and Trevor will never talk to me again."

"He should be here any minute. I called him on the way over and told him we were doing an intervention."

"You're an asshole."

"*Best friend* is the term you're looking for."
"They're often indistinguishable."

"Only if you're doing it right." Dylan touched my arm. "I'm glad you're back, Skye. I'm glad you filled our lake of friendship with ripples."

"*Touching.*"
"You know what I mean."

Squeezing the race car driver in my pocket, I said, "I do. It's good to be back."

"Maybe we're not back. Maybe we're forward."

"You eat too many hash brownies."

"I haven't had a hash brownie in months, thank you very much."

I slumped against the doorway. "I don't want to see Trevor."

"Yeah, you do."

I inhaled sharply and rolled my eyes. "No, I don't. I just keep circling the same place with him."

Dylan ignored me and tilted the empty coffee can on the table. Seeing that it was empty, he raised an eyebrow. "What happened to the chinchilla popsicle?"

Since I hadn't showered in a week and preferred not to be in small spaces with people, I motioned for him to step outside. He followed me around back, where I'd left the shovel leaned against the back wall.

I pointed to where the roof extended over an area of pebbled rocks. "I buried the chinchilla and planted the blueberry bush on top."

"Huh. Two in one. Resourceful." His eyes trailed up to the roof overhead, and then down to the water hose right next to the bush. "Well, it's a good start, I suppose. It needs shade and a lot of water. Did you have a ceremony without me?"

I swallowed. "I think I was so in shock with Stella that I didn't process it. I'm pretty sure I officially buried her when I buried him."

"You could have called me."

"There was a lot of crying."

Dylan shoved his hands in his pockets. "Fair enough." Staring at the blueberry bush, he added, "Though going forward, I'd like for you to act like you know me more. You're so good at making connections, but then you just drop them and walk off. We're going to work on you plugging in. There's real joy in connecting with people and situations, Skye."

"You're proof of that."

My butt-kissing-though-sincere comment made him smile.

"So, tell me about the guy at the funeral."

"The short of it is that he's known my parents forever. He owns a law firm on the edge of town. Stella had a will."

"Really? She never told me that."

"Yeah. Me, neither. Apparently, she only told Mom and Dad."

"So, you don't have to move? Because that makes it easier to find you," he winked.

"I do not have to move. She left Wormy a few things, and me a lot of things."

"How did all that work out?"

"Wormy came over last week."

"Did you shove a shopping cart up her ass?"

"I thought about it, but Wormy is more like me than I'd like to admit. She wished me well with Trevor."

"Huh. What a strange turn of events."

"How's your rock?"

"It positively glows. I think me and the rock have a solid future."

I laughed just as Trevor rounded the back corner of the house. Him seeing me laugh felt like I'd just spit on my sister's urn, awkward and unwelcome.

Trevor glared at me. "So, you probably don't need an intervention."

Dylan gave a strange chuckle. "Don't go for blood so fast, cowboy."

Trevor ignored him. "Nice blueberry bush, Skye."

"Oh, fuck you, Trevor. My sister died."

"*Whoa. Whoa*, guys. Stop. Seriously." Dylan stepped in between us.

"Why'd you call me out here, Dylan?"

"That's not really the question. The real question is: Why did you come?"

"Because I thought you needed help. But Skye is obviously fine. So, I'll be going now."

He looked so sad as he spun around, and so many things rushed through my mind at one time, that I couldn't stop myself from blurting out, "Wait."

Trevor stopped but didn't turn around. "What?"

Dylan stood perfectly still, uncomfortable in the middle. "I'm sorry."

When he didn't move, I thought for a nanosecond he was going to forgive me. Then he walked off. Trevor walking away felt like mountains crumbling.

I was about to go after him when Dylan lurched forward and said, "Hey, buddy. Wait a minute." His Chuck Taylors crunched against the gravel as he sprinted off. By the time I caught up, Trevor was at his truck, hand on the door.

"Wait."

"I already did that for you, Skye."

"Trevor—,"

"I'm absolutely tired of your bullshit, Skye. All the women in my life are raving lunatics who have absolutely no clue what they want, or they die on me. I went to the funeral and put up with you out of respect for Stella, but I don't have to do this."

Standing in the middle of the driveway, twelve feet from an abandoned mouse utopia, I let go of everything I'd been holding so tight for so long. "You're right."

A crack penetrated something deep inside me. I felt like I was falling into oblivion. I honestly didn't care. Oblivion was better than the alternative.

"What does that fix?" Trevor demanded.

"Maybe nothing needs to be fixed," Dylan said. "Maybe we keep misfiring because we're operating under the assumption that everything was broken."

Trevor pointed a finger. "Shut up. You're not helping her out of this with a Zen koan. *Understand?*"

"You're so angry, Trevor."

"Yeah, Skye, I am. And I'm beginning to wonder why you're not angry."

"Because I'm emotionally defunct."

"You're not," Dylan frowned.

"She is," Trevor added.

"Maybe I was. Maybe getting everything I ever wanted terrified me. I wouldn't be alone, and that doesn't excuse it, but it means that sometimes people walk away and leave someone standing in the midday sun because they're confused and naïve and terrified. Maybe I went east because I knew I wasn't whole; knew I was too selfish to ever be good for you. Maybe I went there because I was wrong for you, and I was trying in some awful way to get right."

"Sounds like poetry. *Feels like bullshit.*"

"Nobody is perfect, man," Dylan shrugged.

"You really think you have to say that to me after everything I've been through?"

"I think she burned you, man. I think it pissed you off. I think in a lot of ways you burned each other. But hear me out. I've spent the last few weeks breaking into this house to make sure Skye was okay. And I spent a lot of time thinking about Stella. When she died, I couldn't breathe. I couldn't get air. I obsessed over how I'd always gone with the flow and never made a concrete move, and she was gone. But it was just blind selfishness. Stella was never going to be with me like that. I just couldn't see it. But what comforted me the most was that at least I allowed what we were to each other to exist. At least I didn't spend all my time trying to squeeze her into a box to serve my needs. She was one of my best friends. Literally no one called me on my bullshit like her. But the relationship I thought I was going to have, and the relationship I had, were not the same thing. Not even close."

"I appreciate the fact that you came to terms with the death of our very special friend, but what does that have to do with me?"

"Because, ever since Skye got back, I've watched you two living within the confines of all the relationships you had that didn't work. It's like you're trying to build a new relationship in a swamp. The relationship you two had before didn't work. It's pretty obvious that while you were apart, you spent a lot of time thinking about each other, and that relationship didn't work. Then, Skye came back, and you two sort of fell into this third relationship that is drowning in illusion."

The neighbors stared at all of us in the front yard. I didn't know what to say. For all his TV commercial jingle, sugared cereal, meme-heavy, fortune cookie logic, Dylan was right. I'd spent so much time obsessing over all the things I did wrong, that I couldn't do anything right.

Trevor made eye contact with me.

I did what I'd been thinking about for days. "I want you guys to see something."

CHAPTER TWENTY-SEVEN

Dylan drove because, for some reason, the sensation of us all squeezed into the front seat of his truck was a familiarity we needed. It was a beautiful day. Blue skies fanned out for miles where, just at the horizon, the beginning of sunset teased.

"Are we going for a group session with André?" Trevor asked sarcastically.

I laughed. "No. That never even occurred to me."

"Occurred to me," Trevor said.

I sat straight and still next to him, feeling his arm pressed against mine. I was surprised he even agreed to ride in the same vehicle with me.

Up ahead, I pointed to the entrance of the Sno Cream Castle. "Turn there."

Dylan glanced at me out of the corner of his eye. "Is this going to be a nostalgic trip down memory lane?"

"It's future-forward. I promise."

I'd come from quiet whispers of condolence, sturdy handshakes, pats on the back. I'd come full circle, back to that parking lot.

Dylan parked in-between the faded lines. "So, are we going to hold hands and reminisce?"

Gesturing to the boarded-up front, I said, "I bought it."

"Bought what?" Dylan asked.

"This. I bought a castle."

Trevor laid his hand on his knee and turned to face me. "You're kidding?"

"I'm totally serious."

Dylan turned sideways. "You actually bought this place?"

"Stella bought this place." Tears pushed into my eyes. I'd gone seven hours without crying over my sister and figured that was just going to have to be the world record. I looked at my hands, blurring out of focus. "Stella bought it for me and you," I turned to Trevor, "and you. It's the last thing she did. She signed the paperwork, then went to see Wormy. This is what she was doing before she died."

Trevor looked up into the sky and exhaled.

When the sound of our breathing became too loud to bear, I said, "So, I've been thinking. Maybe we can have frozen yogurt banana splits with organic maple pecan granola, along with blue raspberry pineapple Sno Cones. It's a little hippy-dippy, but it could work."

"Juicy burgers and fries," Dylan said.

"Tempeh strips and curried almond dip," I said.

"Onion rings smothered in barbeque beef," Trevor ventured.

"This might work," Dylan smiled.

It was like a golden metaphor for my life.

This.

Might.

Work.

All of it.

Maybe.

Mostly.

Definitely.

I looked at Trevor. Beyond him was our picnic table, the vast desert sky, the hot temptation of his body under mine. That concrete picnic table was our power spot, our holy ground, our crucifix built for two. I glanced at Dylan. *Okay, crucifix built for three.*

I sat in that moment for a long time, the wash of pink raspberry cantaloupe sky brimming on the horizon. I sat in that moment because it was mine. I'd arrived there. That was my choice. I loved it the way I'd always thought I could love. Holding on and letting go.

Trevor reached for my hand. The warmth of his skin made me melt. A shiver ran down my spine.

What I let hold on to me.

Remember: No one stays in free fall forever.

It just feels that way.

I pulled a single key from my front pocket. The key to an uncertain future.

The paper taped to the windows crinkled when I opened the door. A fine layer of dust sat on top of metal prep tables.

Dylan turned in a complete circle, surveying the front room. "Some of the best moments of my life were created in this place."

"I'm going to create a life for myself in this place," I said quietly.

Trevor exhaled loudly and wrapped his arm around my shoulder. "Deal me in."

That long journey across the desert burned right through me. A transparent hole, where I could finally see I was made of nothingness, and space, and teeny tiny particles of love. In my bravest, darkest times, I'd squeezed my eyes shut to a tender world.

Pulling the Japanese race car driver from my pocket I sat him upright on a metal prep table. "From this we shall rebuild."

Dylan dusted his hands off on his jeans and said, "This calls for a toast."

The long dirt road leading back to Dylan's wound like a snake through the empty stretch of land. Behind craggy mountains, the sun hovered at the edge of darkness. My body leaned forward instinctively. The entire trailer was ablaze with a magnificent pink light seeping out of the cracks. "Welcome to the Jungle" crackled from the old plastic speakers. Buck knocked the door open with his paw and lumbered down the cinder block steps. All that light was swallowed up by all that space, and yet we were closer than we'd ever been.

Years ago, my favorite song was by Dido. Blaring from speakers in gas stations and malls I twirled and sang to everyone who'd listen.

Cue the soundtrack to my life.

Nothing Compares 2 U.

U R A Fever.

Morphine.

Radiohead.

MC Solar.

Toss in some Lauren Hill and fade to end credits.

I loved that day. I'd been coming to it my entire life.

Trevor reached for my hand as Buck whipped his tail back and forth in the driveway. Dylan rolled down his window and whooped.

Stella used to say," Light a candle at the beginning. Extinguish it at the end." It was as close as she ever came to praying. In the front seat, right then, I wanted to thank her for giving me the best day of my life. But mostly, I wanted to look her in the eye just one more time and say:

I'm sorry.
Forgive me.
Thank you.
I love you.

PRAISE FOR OTHER TITLES

Hugely entertaining as well as emotionally moving.
—*Kirkus Reviews*

A delightfully entertaining novel by an author with a genuine flair for originality …
—*Midwest Book Review*

The Wonder Years meets *A Christmas Story* meets *E.T.* in this magical novel ...
—**Cathy Smith Bowers, former Poet Laureate NC**

A loveable, engaging, original voice…
—*Publishers Weekly*

It's a hard book to put down, and one you won't want to end. I envy its future readers.
—*Teresa DiFalco ©2016 Parents' Choice Awards*

ABOUT THE AUTHOR

Hailed as "an author with a genuine flair for originality"
by Midwest Book Review &

"a loveable, engaging, original voice…"
by Publishers Weekly,

Lis Anna-Langston was raised along the winding current of
the Mississippi River on a steady diet of dog-eared books.

You can find her any day of the week in the wilds of South
Carolina plucking stories out of thin air.

If you loved this title please leave a review & follow
Lis Anna-Langston on insta **@lis.anna.langston**
Let's connect **www.lisannalangston.com** to get on the
Lis(t)
& stay in touch.

www.ingramcontent.com/pod-product-compliance
Lightning Source LLC
Chambersburg PA
CBHW052024240626
47153CB00006B/1937